INTRODUCTION

Fascinated as he was by every branch of science, Jules Verne could not but be interested in the controversy over the Darwinian Theory which was raging during his lifetime. As at the same time he was a sincerely religious man, and followed faithfully the teachings of the Roman Catholic Church, he naturally regarded the extremists of the Evolutionary School of thought with a certain scepticism.

At that time the controversy almost turned upon the possible existence of a "Missing Link," a creature intermediate between man and the anthropoid apes. Was there any such creature? Or was the gulf between the animals and man complete and unbridgeable? His story might be regarded as a somewhat inconclusive suggestion of the manner in which the problem might be solved, and he leaves the reader to form his own conclusions.

This remarkable story, which has apparently never hitherto been translated into English, was originally entitled *Le Village Aérien*. This, however, especially as connected with the name of Jules Verne, would rather suggest some sort of super flying-machine, and it is for this reason I have given it a different title, which I think conveys its theme more clearly. My only other alteration is the omission of a few short passages of minor interest, mostly consisting of geographical detail now completely out of date.

I.O.E.

Rick Colyer

This is the first English translation of one of the last of Jules Verne's works to be published in his own lifetime. Set in the heart of Africa, it is the story of two ivory hunters, accompanied by a young African boy. When their caravan is attacked and destroyed by a herd of wild elephants, they have to proceed on foot, firstly through jungle, and then down river by raft. Unexplained lights are seen moving among the treetops at the river's edge, and then the travellers come across an overhanging cage. Inside, they find the note-books of a German professor, who has been studying the great apes, apparently with the idea of learning their 'language'. The professor himself has disappeared, though whether he has been killed or carried off by the apes is not known.

The native boy finds an untended baby monkey; but is it a monkey? The boy swears that he has heard it utter an articulate word; it has called, in an African dialect, for its mother.

Has the party come across the much-fabled 'missing link'? No Darwinian, Verne's answer is as intriguing as the rest of his story.

JULES VERNE, recognized as the founder of modern science-fiction, was born in Nantes, France, on Feb. 8, 1828, and died in Amiens on March 24, 1905. He was educated in Nantes and later in Paris, where he went with the intention of taking up the law. However, his natural penchant for storytelling caused the abandonment of that study in favor of recounting the marvels of the universe.

It was in 1858 that his first efforts appeared, in the form of travel stories in magazines. Then, in 1862, his first successful novel, *Five Weeks in a Balloon,* launched the series his publisher entitled "Les Voyages Extraordinaires". The second of this series was *Journey to the Center of the Earth,* which appeared in 1864, and which brought its author world fame and immediate popularity. Verne produced a new work of science-fiction or astonishing adventure every year thereafter, ever increasing his following until his works were known all over the world and selling in the millions. Among his best-known novels are *From the Earth to the Moon, Around the World in Eighty Days, Twenty Thousand Leagues Under the Sea,* and *The Mysterious Island.*

Verne's gift for prophecy was always based upon a sound scientific foundation which has earned for him a literary permanence often lacking in his imitators or successors.

JULES VERNE

The Village In The Treetops

Translated from the French by I. O. EVANS

ACE BOOKS, INC.
1120 Avenue of the Americas
New York, N.Y. 10036

THE VILLAGE IN THE TREETOPS

Copyright ©, 1964, by Arco Publications

An Ace Book, by arrangement with Associated Booksellers.

Originally published in French in 1901 under the title
Le Village Aérien

Cover art by Jerome Podwil; sketch of Verne by Ron Miller.

Printed in U.S.A.

THE VILLAGE IN THE TREETOPS

nothing to desire from the point of view of solidity. After the trials of that long and painful expedition, its body in good condition, its wheels with their felloes hardly worn, its axles unbroken and unbent, it looked as if it had returned from a mere drive of fifteen to twenty leagues, although it had covered more than twelve hundred miles.

Three months previously, this vehicle had left Libreville, the capital of the French Congo. Thence, travelling eastwards, it had gone further into the Oubanghi than the course of the Behar-el-Abiad, one of the tributaries which pour their water into the southern part of Lake Chad.

It is to one of the principal tributaries on the right bank of the Congo that this country owes its name. It extends to the east of the German Cameroons, and its boundary is not clearly marked on any of the maps, not even on the most modern. If it is not actually a desert—for it has a flourishing vegetation and does not in any way resemble the Sahara—it is at least a vast wilderness over which a few lonely villages are scattered.

Its peoples are continually at war, enslaving or killing one another, and living on human flesh. And, what is worst of all, these cannibalistic instincts are usually satisfied on the children. The missionaries, therefore, devote themselves to saving these tiny creatures, either by carrying them off by force or by ransoming them, and they give them a Christian education in the Missions founded along the river Siramba. But it must not be forgotten that these Missions would soon fail for lack of funds if the generosity of the European countries, and especially that of France, were to cease.

It must be added that in this region the children are regarded as the small change in trading. The foodstuffs which the traders are bringing right into the heart of the country are paid for in small boys and little girls. So the richest native is the one with the largest family.

But if the Portuguese Urdax was not venturing across

these plains purely for commercial reasons, if he had no trade with the tribes along the Oubanghi, if he had no other object than to get supplies of ivory by chasing the elephant so abundant in this region, he had not failed to make contact with the fierce peoples of the Congo. In several encounters he had had to make these hostile tribes respect him and to transform into defensive weapons against the natives the guns which he had meant to use in chasing the herds of elephants.

But on the whole it had been a fortunate and rewarding journey, which had not counted even one victim among the personnel of the caravan.

And, just on the borders of a village near the courses of the Behar-el-Abiad, John Cort and Max Huber had been able to snatch a child from the dreadful fate which awaited him and to ransom him at the cost of a handful of beads. He was a small boy about ten years old, strong, and with an interesting face, which showed little of the Negro type. As may be seen amongst some of these tribes, he had almost a light complexion, fair hair instead of the crisp wool of the Negroes, an aquiline unflattened nose; nor did he have the thick Negroid lips. His eyes shone with intelligence and he felt for those who had saved him a sort of filial affection.

This poor child, carried off from his tribe, if not from his family—for he had neither father nor mother—was called Llanga. After having been educated by the Missionaries, who had taught him a little French and English, he had had the bad luck to fall into the hands of the Denkas, and it may well be guessed what fate awaited him. Attracted by his affection, by the gratitude he showed them, the two friends had got very fond of the child; they fed and clothed him and they educated him very profitably, for he showed a precocious intelligence.

And then, what a difference for Llanga! Instead of being, like those unfortunate native youngsters, turned into a sort of living merchandise, he lived in the factories

THE VILLAGE IN THE TREETOPS

of Libreville, he became the adopted child of Max Huber and John Cort . . . they had taken charge of him and they would never forsake him! . . . In spite of his youth, he realised this, he felt himself loved, and a tear of happiness rolled from his eyes every time that the hands of either of his two friends were laid on his head.

When the wagon had stopped, the bullocks, wearied by a long journey through an atrocious heat, lay down on the grass. At once Llanga, who had been going on foot during part of the journey, sometimes ahead of and sometimes behind the team, ran up at the very moment when his two protectors stepped on to the ground.

"You're not too tired, Llanga?" asked John Cort, as he grasped the boy's hand.

"No . . . no! . . . good legs . . . and much like running," Llanga replied, smiling with lips and eyes at his two friends.

"Now it's time to eat!" Max Huber told him.

"To eat . . . Yes . . . my friend Max!"

Then, after kissing the hands which were held out to him, he went off to join the porters beneath the shade of the great trees on the mound.

If the wagon was used only to carry the Portuguese Urdax, Khamis, and their two companions, it was because the baggage and the loads of ivory had been entrusted to the personnel of the caravan—about fifty men, mostly blacks from the Cameroons. They had deposited on the ground the elephant tusks and the boxes which assured their daily food, apart from that obtained by hunting in the game-rich region of the Oubanghi.

These natives were only hirelings, trained for the work and paid well enough for them to benefit from the results of the expeditions. One might even say that they had never "hatched their eggs" to use the term by which the natives describe the stay-at-homes. Accustomed from their childhood to be porters, they would go on being porters until their legs gave way under them. Nonetheless their task was hard, having to be carried out in such a climate, their shoulders bending beneath the heavy ivory of the weighty boxes of provisions, their skins chafed by the coarse undergrowth, for they went almost naked, and their feet bleeding, they journeyed from dawn to eleven in the morning and went on until evening as soon as the heat of the day had passed.

But in their own interests the merchants had to see that these men were well paid, and they were well paid; that they should be well looked after, and they were well looked after; that they should not be driven beyond all reason, and they were not over-driven. The perils of elephant-hunting were very real, not to speak of the chance of meeting lions or panthers, and the leader had to be able to count on his personnel.

Moreover, the harvest of precious material having been reaped, it was important for the caravan to be able to return peaceably and quickly to the factories on the coast. So it was profitable for it not to be held up by delays caused by excessive fatigue or illness—especially by smallpox, whose ravages were most to be dreaded. Steeped in these principles, and taught by long experience, Urdax took the greatest care of his men and had succeeded in making lucrative expeditions into the heart of equatorial Africa.

This last expedition was among them, for it had brought a good store of high-quality ivory, gathered from the districts beyond the Behar-el-Abiad, almost on the boundary of Darfour.

It was under the shade of some splendid tamarisk trees that the camp was set up. When, after the porters had started unpacking the provisions, John Cort questioned Urdax, he got the following reply, in the English which the Portuguese could speak fluently: "Mr. Cort, I think this is quite a convenient place to make a halt, and the table is all laid for our cattle."

"Certainly, they'll have plenty of good thick grass," John agreed. "And anybody would be glad to eat it,"

THE VILLAGE IN THE TREETOPS

Max Huber added. "If he were built like a ruminant and had three stomachs to digest it with!"

"Thanks," John Cort replied, "but I'd rather have an antelope steak grilled on the coals, the biscuits that we've got so many of, and some of our Cape Madeira."

"We could add a few drops from this clear stream which is flowing across the plain," commented the Portuguese.

And he pointed to a rivulet—no doubt a tributary of the Oubanghi—flowing half a mile away from the hillock.

The camp was set up without delay, and the ivory was piled up in heaps near the wagon, while the cattle wandered about among the trees. Fires were kindled with the fallen wood, and the foreloper made sure that the different groups lacked nothing. Eland and antelope meat, dried or fresh, was there in abundance, and the hunters would easily be able to replace it. The air was filled with the fragrance of grilled meat, and each of the men showed a formidable appetite, justified by half a day's trekking.

It goes without saying that the arms and ammunitions were ready in the wagon—several cases of cartridges, shotguns, carbines, revolvers, splendid weapons of the most modern type for use by the three white men and Khamis in case of an alarm.

Half an hour later the meal was over. Their stomachs satisfied, and weariness aiding, the caravan was not slow in being plunged into a deep slumber.

All the same, the foreloper trusted in the watchfulness of several of his men, who were to relieve one another every two hours. In these remote parts it was essential to guard against creatures with evil intentions, whether on four feet or two. So Urdax did not fail to take all the steps which prudence demanded.

About fifty years old but still vigorous, well accustomed to leading expeditions of this kind, he was able to show extraordinary endurance. Similarly Khamis, thirty-five years old, brisk, active, very cool and very brave, could offer every guarantee for guiding a caravan across Africa.

It was at the foot of one of the tamarisks that the two friends and the native had sat down to supper, brought to them by the boy and prepared by the Negro who had been entrusted with the duties of cook.

During the meal tongues were not idle any more than jaws were. Eating does not hinder talking, so long as one is not in a hurry. What were they talking about? . . . The incidents they had encountered during their expedition? . . . Not a bit of it. What might happen on the way back was of more immediate interest. It was still a long journey to the Libreville factories—more than twelve hundred miles away—and it would take nine or ten weeks. And during that second half of the journey, who knows? —as John Cort had pointed out to his companion, who was looking out for something unforeseen and quite out of the ordinary.

To reach this last stage, beyond the limits of Darfour, the caravan had redescended towards the Oubanghi, after crossing the fords of the Aoukadébé and its numerous tributaries. That day they had halted where the twenty-second meridian meets the ninth parallel.

"But now," said Urdax, "we ought to go off towards the south-west."

"And what makes that plain," John Cort replied, "if my eyes aren't deceiving me, is that towards the south the horizon is barred by a forest, and I can't see its end towards either the east or the west."

"Yes . . . it's immense!" the Portuguese agreed, "if we had to skirt round the east side it would take months to get beyond it."

"While if we go westwards? . . ."

"Going westwards," Urdax replied, "and following the edge of the forest, so as not to lengthen our journey more than we can help, we should reach the Oubanghi somewhere near the Zongo rapids."

THE VILLAGE IN THE TREETOPS

"Wouldn't it shorten the journey if we went through it," asked Max Huber.

"Yes, by about fifteen days march."

"Then why don't we go straight through it?"

"Because it's impenetrable."

"Oh, impenetrable." Max Huber spoke in tones which lacked conviction.

"Not on foot, perhaps," commented the Portuguese, "but I can't even be certain of that, because nobody's tried it. But to try to get the cattle through it, that would be to try something that wouldn't get us anywhere."

"You say, Urdax, that nobody has ever tried to get through that forest?"

"Tried . . . well, I don't know, Mr. Max, but that anyone's ever succeeded . . . no . . . and in the Cameroons as in the Congo anyone would be ill-advised to try it. Who could expect to get through there, where there's no footpath at all, in the midst of thorn-covered thickets and bushes? I doubt if a way could be cut through them even with fire and axes—to say nothing of the dead trees, which would form an insurmountable obstacle."

"Insurmountable, Urdax?"

"Look, my friend," broke in John Cort, "don't try and get mixed up in that forest, and be thankful you've only got to go round it. I must say I shouldn't like to enter into such a maze of trees!"

"Not even to know what's inside it?"

"And what do you expect to find inside it, Max? Unknown kingdoms, enchanted cities, mythological eldorados, new kinds of animals and human beings with three legs?"

"Why not, John? . . . All we've got to do is to go and look!"

Llanga, looking on with wide open eyes and excitement written on his face, seemed to be saying that if Max Huber were to venture into that wood, he would not be afraid to follow him.

"Anyhow," continued John Cort, "as Urdax has no intention of going through it to reach the banks of the Oubanghi . . ."

"No, indeed," replied the Portuguese, "that would be to take the chance of never coming out!"

"Well, my dear Max, let's have a nap, and you'll be welcome to go and look for mysteries in that forest, to endanger yourself in those impenetrable thickets . . . but only in your dreams, and even then you wouldn't be too safe."

"That's right, John, laugh at me as much as you like! But I remember what one of our poets said. . . . I don't know which:

"Fouiller dans l'inconnu pour trouver du nouveau."*

"Really, Max . . . and what's the line that rhymes with that?"

"My word, John . . . I've completely forgotten it!"

"Then forget the first line just as you've forgotten the second, and let's go to sleep."

That was plainly the wisest thing to do—and there was no need to shelter in the wagon. A night at the foot of the hillock, beneath those great tamarisks whose freshness might temper the surrounding heat, still oppressive after sunset, that would not worry men who were accustomed "to do star-pitch under the blue blanket"† whenever the weather permitted. That evening, although the stars were hidden behind thick clouds, there was no risk of rain and it would be better to sleep in the open.

The young native brought them their sleeping-bags, and soon the two friends, snugly wrapped up, stretched themselves out between the roots of a tamarisk—a regular open-air shelter—while Llanga crouched down beside

---

*"To plunge into the unknown to find something new."

†"Dormir à l'hotel de la Belle Etoile."

THE VILLAGE IN THE TREETOPS

them like a watchdog. Before following their example, Urdax and Khamis went round the camp for the last time, making certain that the cattle were hobbled and could not stray over the plain, that the porters were on the look-out, and that the fires had been extinguished, for one spark would be enough to kindle the dry grass and the dead wood. Then they returned to the hillock.

Sleep was not long in embracing them—a sleep so profound they would not have heard it thunder—and as for the sentinels, perhaps they too had been overcome by weariness? . . . Indeed, after ten o'clock there was nobody to notice the suspicious-looking flames which were moving about on the edge of the great forest.

CHAPTER II

THE MOVING FLAMES

A DISTANCE of about a mile and half at most separated the hillock from the vague shadows at whose foot these flashing wavering flames were going to and fro. About ten of them might have been counted, now together, now separating, sometimes flickering with a violence incompatible with the calmness of the air. It seemed likely that a horde of natives was encamped at that place and waiting for dawn.

Yet the fires were not those of a camp. Instead of being grouped together as though forming the centre for a night's halt, they were coming and going at random over a distance of about two hundred yards.

It must be borne in mind that the Oubanghi country was the haunt of nomadic tribes, coming from the east or from the west. A trading caravan would not have been

JULES VERNE

so unwise as to announce its presence by a number of flames moving about among the shadows. Only natives would have halted at such a place. And who could tell whether they might not have hostile intentions against the caravan asleep under the shade of the tamarisks?

Whatever the facts—if indeed some danger were menacing the caravan, if several hundred fierce natives were awaiting the moment to attack it with the advantage of superior numbers—nobody—at least before half past ten—had taken any defensive measures. Everybody in the camp was asleep, masters and servants alike; and, what was more serious, the porters on duty at the look-out posts were also plunged into a heavy slumber.

Fortunately the small boy awoke and no doubt his eyes had not been fully closed when they turned towards the south. Through his half-closed eyelids he got the impression of a light piercing the darkness of night. He stretched himself, he rubbed his eyes, he looked more carefully. . . . No, he was not mistaken; there were scattered flames moving about at the edge of the forest.

Rather by instinct than by reason, Llanga jumped to the conclusion that the caravan was about to be attacked. Certainly anyone preparing for murder and pillage would be bound to know that his chances would be greatly improved by a surprise attack. Such people would not let themselves be seen prematurely and they might be signalling to one another? . . .

Not wanting to disturb either of his friends, the boy climbed silently into the wagon. When he reached the foreloper he aroused him by gripping his shoulder: then he pointed to the fires on the horizon.

As soon as Khamis saw the moving flames he called Urdax in a voice which he did not trouble to keep low.

Accustomed to free himself at short notice from the mists of sleep, the Portuguese was on his feet in an instant: "What's up, Khamis?"

"Look!" and with outstretched arm the foreloper pointed across the plain to the flame-lit edge of the forest.

THE VILLAGE IN THE TREETOPS

"Look out!" the Portuguese shouted with all the strength of his lungs.

In a few seconds the whole personnel of the caravan were on their feet. So preoccupied were they with the danger of the position that nobody thought about blaming the careless sentries. But for Llanga, it seemed likely that the whole caravan would have been attacked while Urdax and his companions were asleep.

It goes without saying that Max Huber and John Cort, hurriedly leaving their shelter between the tree-roots, had joined the Portuguese and the foreloper.

It was a little after half past ten. In three directions, north, east, and west, thick darkness covered the plain. Only to the south there gleamed these torch-like flames, emitting gleams of brightness as they moved to and fro and numbering not less than fifty.

"It must be a whole crowd of the natives," said Urdax, "probably one of those tribes who live beside the Congo and the Oubanghi."

"To be sure," Khamis added, "those fires didn't light themselves."

"And," commented John Cort, "there must be arms to move them about."

"But," Max Huber pointed out, "those arms must be attached to shoulders and those shoulders to bodies, and yet in spite of the illumination we can't see even one of them. . . ."

"That may be because they're just inside the wood behind the trees," Khamis suggested.

"And we can see," Max Huber continued, "that it's not a question of a tribe on the march along the edge of the forest . . . No, though these fires keep spreading out to right and left, they always return to the same spot."

"So that's where their camp must be," the foreloper declared.

"What do you think?" John Cort asked Urdax.

"I think we're going to be attacked, and that we'd better get ready to defend ourselves without delay."

"But why didn't they attack us before showing themselves?"

"Blacks aren't whites," the Portuguese replied, "all the same they're being so rash doesn't make them any the less formidable, what with their numbers and their ferocious instinct."

"Panthers which our missionaries will find it hard to turn into lambs!" was Max Huber's comment.

"Let's get ready for them!" the Portuguese advised.

Yes, get ready to defend themselves, and to defend themselves to the last. No mercy was to be hoped for from the tribes of the Oubanghi. Nobody knew what limits there might be to their cruelty, and the fiercest tribes of Australia or of the South Sea Islands, would be hard to compare with these natives. Towards the centre of the region there are nothing but cannibal villages, and the Fathers of the Mission, who dare the most frightful of deaths, have some reason to know it. In this equatorial Africa where strength is everything and weakness is a crime, one feels inclined to class such beings, wild beasts with human faces, among the animals! Moreover, even in maturity few of these natives can boast even the vestiges of the intelligence of a child of five or six.

And it may safely be said—there is an abundant proof of this, for the missionaries have often witnessed the most frightful scenes—that human sacrifice is general in this country. Slaves are killed on their master's tombs, and their heads, tied on to bent branches, are hurled afar as soon as they have been severed by the witch-doctor's knife. At the formal ceremonies, children of from ten to sixteen serve as the food, and some of the chiefs live entirely on their young flesh.

To these cannibalistic instincts are joined those of plunder. This sometimes brings the tribes from afar on to the routes of the caravans—these they attack, pillage, and destroy. Though less well-armed than the merchants and their personnel, they outnumber them, and thousands of

THE VILLAGE IN THE TREETOPS

natives can always get the better of the few hundred porters.

The forelopers are well aware of this. So one of their chief aims is not to get involved among these villages, where the missionaries have not yet appeared but which they will one day reach. No terrors restrain the devotion of these gallant men when there is need to rescue the little ones from death and to regenerate the savage tribes by the influence of Christian civilisation.

Since the expedition had started out, Urdax had not always been able to avoid attack by the natives, but he had invariably extricated himself without much damage, and he still kept the whole of his personnel.

The return journey looked like being carried out in complete safety. The forest skirted on the west, they would reach the right bank of the Oubanghi and descend it until it debouched into the Congo. Beyond that point the country is frequented by merchants and missionaries. Thenceforward the travellers would have less to fear from contact with the nomadic tribes which, through the initiative of the European nations are being driven back towards the distant lands of the Darfour.

But, as several days' march was needed to reach the river, might not the caravan be halted on its way, find itself at grips with so many robbers that it would at last be overcome? . . . Whatever happened, it would not perish for want of resistance, and at the command of the Portuguese steps were taken to organise the defence.

He himself, with the foreloper, John Cort and Max Huber, were at once armed, carbines in hand, revolvers in their belts, their cartridge-belts well filled. The wagon contained a dozen or so rifles and pistols, and these were confided to several of the porters who were known to be trustworthy.

At the same time Urdax ordered his men to take their places among the great tamarisks, so as to find shelter from the arrows, whose poisoned tips could inflict mortal wounds.

JULES VERNE

They waited. No sound reached them. The natives did not seem to have advanced beyond the forest. The flames were still burning incessantly, and here and there rose long streams of yellow smoke.

"Those must be resinous torches moving about on the edge of the trees."

"That's right," Max Huber agreed, "but I still can't make out why those fellows are doing that if they're going to attack us. . . ."

"And I can't make it out either," added John Cort, "if they're not going to."

It was certainly inexplicable. But all the same, why should anyone be surprised at anything the moment those brutes from the upper Oubanghi were involved? . . .

Half an hour elapsed without bringing any change in the situation. The camp kept on the alert. While those fires were gleaming southwards, a detachment could glide through the darkness to attack the caravan on its flank. In that direction the plain was obviously deserted. Dark though the night was, no group of assailants could surprise the Portuguese and his comrades before the latter could use their weapons.

A little later, towards eleven, Max Huber, going a few steps away from the others, said in firm tones, "Let's go and have a look at them."

"Is that worth while?" asked John Cort, "wouldn't it be more prudent to keep on the look-out until daybreak?"

"Wait! . . . wait! . . ." replied Max Huber. "After our sleep has been so annoyingly interrupted . . . wait another six or seven hours, with our fingers on the trigger! . . . No, we've got to know what's happening before that! . . . And indeed, if those natives aren't plotting any mischief, I shan't be sorry to curl up in that niche among the roots where I was having such lovely dreams!"

"What do you think?" John Cort asked the Portuguese, who had kept silent.

"Maybe the idea ought to be acted on," he replied, "but don't let's act carelessly."

THE VILLAGE IN THE TREETOPS

"I'm willing to go out scouting," Max Huber volunteered, "and you can trust me...."

"I'll go with you," said the foreloper, "if Mr. Urdax agrees."

"That would certainly be better," the Portuguese assented.

"I could come with you too . . ." suggested John Cort.

"No, stay here, my dear fellow," Max Huber insisted, "two will be quite enough. Besides, we shan't go any further than we have to. And if we don't come across anyone approaching from that side, we'll hurry back."

"Take care your weapons are ready," John Cort reminded them.

"That's done," replied Khamis, "but we shan't have to use them. The great thing is to keep out of sight."

"That's my opinion," the Portuguese declared.

Max Huber and the foreloper, keeping close together, were soon beyond the hillock. Here the plain seemed rather less dark, but still a man would not be visible a hundred paces away.

They had scarcely gone fifty yards when they saw Llanga behind them. The boy had followed them from the camp without a word.

"Well, what have you come for child?" asked Khamis.

"Yes, Llanga," agreed Max Huber, "why didn't you stay with the others?"

"Go on, get back," were the foreloper's orders.

"Oh, Mr. Max," Llanga murmured, "with you . . . me . . . with you."

"But you know quite well that your friend John is there."

"Yes . . . but my friend Max . . . is here."

"We don't want you," Khamis told him somewhat harshly.

"Let him stay now he is here," was Max Huber's advice, "he won't hinder us, Khamis, and with his eyes like a wild cat's he may be able to notice something in the gloom that we can't see."

25

JULES VERNE

"Yes . . . I'll look out . . . I'll look far," the boy assured them.

"That's fine!" said Max Huber, "keep close to me and keep your eyes open!"

All three went forward. A quarter of an hour later they were about half-way between the camp and the great forest.

The flames were still throwing out their light at the foot of the trees, and now that they were less distant they appeared more vividly. But however far-sighted the foreloper was, however good were the field-glasses which Max Huber had just taken from their case, however piercing were the eyes of the young "wild cat," they could not make out what it was that was moving the torches about.

This confirmed the view of the Portuguese that their movements were going on under cover of the forest, behind the thick undergrowth and the tall trees. Certainly the natives had not left the edge of the forest and perhaps they did not mean to.

Things were really getting more and more inexplicable. If nothing were happening except that the Negroes had halted for the night, with the idea of pushing on again next morning, why this illumination of the edge of the forest? What nocturnal ceremony was being performed at this hour of the night? . . .

"And I'd like to know," added Max Huber, "if they saw our caravan, and if they realise that we're encamped among the tamarisks?"

"Maybe," replied Khamis, "if they got here only at nightfall when dusk had already covered the plain and our fires had been put out, perhaps they don't know that we're encamped so near. But at dawn tomorrow they'll see us."

"Provided we haven't pushed on, Khamis."

Max Huber and the foreloper went on in silence.

Another quarter of a mile was covered, reducing their distance from the forest to a few hundred yards.

THE VILLAGE IN THE TREETOPS

There was nothing suspicious on the surface of the ground now lit up by the torches. No shadow appeared upon it, neither to the south, the east, nor the west. No immediate attack seemed likely. Nevertheless, near though they were to the wood, neither of them could make out the creatures who showed their presence by these many flames.

"Ought we to go any nearer?" Max Huber asked after a few moments' pause.

"What's the use?" replied Khamis. "Wouldn't that be risky? Quite possibly, after all, our camp hasn't been seen, and if we set off in the middle of the night . . ."

"All the same I'd like to make certain," Max Huber insisted. "This is all so extraordinary."

It would not have taken as much as this to arouse the Frenchman's imagination. "Let's get back to the hillock," was the foreloper's advice, but all the same, he had to follow Max a little further forward, while Llanga would not leave him. And they might have gone right up to the edge of the forest had not Khamis stopped suddenly.

"Not a step further!" he whispered.

Was it some imminent danger which made them come to a halt? . . . Had they spotted a group of natives? . . . Were they going to be attacked? . . . Only one thing was certain, that a sudden change had just taken place in the arrangement of the lights at the edge of the forest.

A moment later, and those lights had disappeared behind the curtain of the first trees and were lost in the darkness.

"Look out!" exclaimed Max Huber.

"Back!" Khamis ordered.

Should they retreat at the threat of an immediate attack? Anyhow, it would be better not to have to fight a delaying action without being ready to return blow for blow. The loaded carbines rose to their shoulders, while their gaze never stopped trying to probe the dark shadows along the edge of the forest.

JULES VERNE

Suddenly, in those shadows, more of the lights, about a score in number, suddenly flared up.

"Well," exclaimed Max Huber, "if that isn't extraordinary, at least it's rather queer!"

The words seemed appropriate, for the torches, after gleaming almost at ground level were now emitting brighter rays between fifty and a hundred feet above the ground.

As to the beings, whoever they were, who were waving these torches, now near the ground, now near the treetops, neither of the onlookers could make out even one of them.

"Well," said Huber again, "aren't they will-of-the-wisps dancing about among the trees?"

Khamis shook his head; he did not find the explanation satisfactory. There might possibly have been some escape of jets of flaming hydrogen. But a score of those gleams which thunderstorms can produce on tree-branches as well as on the masts of ships, no, certainly not—and these flames could not possibly be confused with the wayward gleam of the St. Elmo's Fire. The air was not charged with electricity, and the clouds were threatening to empty themselves in one of those torrential rains which often deluge the central part of the Dark Continent.

Still, why had the natives climbed from their camp at the foot of the trees up to the forks and even to the ends of the branches? . . . And why were they carrying those burning brands, those resinous torches whose crackling could be heard even at such a distance? . . .

"Let's get on," said Max Huber.

"No use," replied the foreloper. "I don't think our camp is threatened tonight, and we'd better get back to reassure our comrades."

"We'll be able to reassure them better, Khamis, when we know the meaning of all this."

"No, Mr. Max, we mustn't go any further. It's certain that a whole tribe is there . . . Why have these wanderers lighted their flames? . . . Why have they taken refuge in the treetops? . . . Was it to frighten away the wild beasts that they lit their fires? . . ."

"Wild beasts?" Max Huber replied. "But panthers, hyenas, wild oxen—we'd have heard them roaring or bellowing, and the only sound we can hear is the crackling of that resin, which must be threatening to set fire to the forest! . . . I want to find out . . ."

And, followed by Llanga, he went on a few paces, while Khamis vainly called after him.

Unable to restrain the impatient Frenchman, the foreloper was uncertain what to do. However, not wishing to let him go on alone, he was about to accompany him towards the trees, though this in his opinion, was an unpardonable rashness.

Suddenly he paused, just as Max Huber and Llanga likewise stopped, and all three turned their backs on the forest. But it was no longer the flames that attracted their attention: as at the gust of a sudden storm, the torches had just gone out, and complete darkness reached as far as the horizon.

From the other side a distant noise could be heard coming through the air. Or rather, it was a concert of prolonged bellowings, of nasal roarings, suggesting that some gigantic organ was hurling its powerful notes across the plain.

Was it a storm arising in that part of the sky, and disturbing the air with its first mutterings? . . .

No, it was not another of those atmospheric disturbances which so often spread desolation from coast to coast across equatorial Africa. These characteristic bellowings betrayed their animal origin and could not come from the echoes of bursts of thunder in the depths of the sky. They must be coming not from electric clouds but from formidable throats. Nor were the low-lying clouds streaked with exploding zig-zags following one another at short intervals. Not a flash above the northern horizon, which was as dark as that of the south. Not a gleam of fire between the clouds piled up like whorls of smoke.

"What's this, Khamis?" asked Max Huber.

"Back to the camp!" shouted the foreloper.

"What can it be?" Max repeated.

And, stretching his ears in that direction, he heard more clearly a sound like a trumpet, but as strident as a whistle of a locomotive, in the midst of a great rumbling which grew ever louder as it approached them.

"Let's be off," commanded the foreloper, "and as fast as we can!"

CHAPTER III

SCATTERED

It did not take them ten minutes to cross the mile which separated them from the hillock. They did not once look round, not troubling to find out if the natives, after extinguishing their flames, were trying to follow them. No, on that side peace reigned, whereas in the other direction the plain seemed filled with confused movements and a startling din.

When the three reached it, the camp was overcome with fear—a fear justified by the threat of a peril against which neither courage nor skill could prevail. To face it was impossible. But to escape? . . . Would there be time? . . . Max Huber and Khamis at once joined John Cort and Urdax, who had taken up their position fifty paces away from the hillock.

"A herd of elephants!" the foreloper exclaimed.

"Yes," replied the Portuguese, "and in less than a quarter of an hour they'll be upon us."

"Let's make for the forest!" suggested John Cort.

"It won't be the forest that will stop them," Khamis objected.

THE VILLAGE IN THE TREETOPS

"What's become of the natives?" Cort wanted to know.
"We haven't seen them anywhere," Huber replied.
"But they won't have left the forest!"
"Certainly not."

A little over a mile and a half away they could make out a mass of moving shadows about two hundred yards wide. It was like a gigantic wave whose chaotic crests were noisily breaking. A heavy trampling was being transmitted across the elastic layers of soil, and its effect could be felt at the very roots of the tamarisks. Meanwhile the roaring had attained a frightful intensity. Strident breathings, metallic blasts, were being emitted by those hundred of trunks, like bugles blown with all the strength of the lungs.

Travellers in central Africa have compared this noise to that of a column of artillery rolling at full speed across the battlefield. Agreed! But on condition that the trumpeters were hurling their strident notes into the air. It is easy to imagine the terror which gripped the caravan's personnel, faced with the threat of being wiped out by this herd of elephants!

Hunting these gigantic beasts offers serious difficulties. When one of them can be surprised alone, can be separated from the herd to which it belongs, when it is possible to fire under conditions which will ensure that the bullet will find its mark in the one place, between the eye and the ear, where it kills instantaneously, the dangers of the hunt are greatly reduced. Where a herd consists only of a few animals, the most stringent precautions, the most exacting prudence, are essential.

Against a dozen infuriated elephants no resistance is possible, for, as the mathematicians say, their mass is multiplied by the square of their velocity. And if these formidable beasts hurl themselves on a camp by hundreds, they can no more be checked in their career than an avalanche, or than one of those tidal-waves which carry ships inland to a distance of several miles from the coast.

During their expedition the Portuguese had had reason to congratulate himself, as had the two lovers of hunting, for the elephants are still numerous on the Libyan continent. The Oubanghi regions offer them the habitat they seek, the forests and marshy plains they love. They live in herds, normally watched over by an old male. By luring them into stockaded enclosures, by laying traps for them, by attacking them when they were alone, Urdax and his companions had had a prosperous journey, without accident if not without peril or fatigue. But during this return journey did it not seem that this furious herd, whose cries were still rending the air, was going to crush in its onset the whole caravan? . . .

Even if the Portuguese had had time to organise the defence when he had feared an attack by the natives encamped on the edge of the forest, what could he have done against this onrush? . . . Of the whole encampment there would remain nothing but fragments and dust! . . . The whole question came to this: would the personnel succeed in reaching safety by scattering over the plain? What could not be forgotten was that the speed of an elephant is amazing, and that a galloping horse cannot overtake it.

"We must run . . . run at once!" Khamis told the Portuguese.

"Run!" Urdax protested. The unhappy hunter knew only too well that this would mean losing all the profits of the expedition as well as his equipment.

Yet to stay in camp, would that save him, and would it not be madness to insist upon carrying on an impossible resistance? . . . Max Huber and John Cort waited for a decision to be reached, and made up their minds, whatever it was, to conform to it.

But the herd was approaching and creating such an uproar that they could hardly succeed in making themselves heard.

The foreloper repeated that they must get away at once.

THE VILLAGE IN THE TREETOPS

"Which way?" asked Max Huber.

"Towards the forest."

"What about the natives?"

"There's less danger there than there is here!" Khamis replied.

How could they be sure of that? But one thing at least was certain, that they could not stay where they were. The only way to escape being wiped out was to seek refuge in the forest.

But would they have time? Over a mile to go, while the herd were barely half that distance away!

They were all waiting for orders from Urdax, orders which he did not seem inclined to give. At last he shouted: "The wagon; ... the wagon! ... put it in shelter behind the tree! Perhaps it will be safe there!"

"Too late," replied the foreloper.

"Do what I tell you!" the Portuguese ordered.

"How?" asked Khamis.

Indeed, after having broken the hobbles, without which they could not be stopped, the draught-oxen had made off, running just ahead of that monstrous herd which would crush them like flies.

On seeing this, Urdax tried to appeal to its personnel: "This way, porters!" he shouted.

"Porters?" asked Khamis. "You'd better call them back, for they've made off too."

"The cowards!" exclaimed John Cort.

Yes, all the Negroes had made off towards the west of the camp, some carrying away their bundles and others the tusks. They were forsaking their masters not only as cowards but as thieves!

These men could not be relied on. They would never return. They would find a refuge in the native villages. Of the whole caravan there remained only the Portuguese and the foreloper, the Frenchman, the American, and the small boy.

"The wagon ... the wagon!" Urdax repeated, anxious to shelter it behind the hillock.

JULES VERNE

Khamis could not keep from shrugging his shoulders. But nevertheless he obeyed, and thanks to the help of the others, the wagon was pushed to the foot of the trees. Perhaps it would be spared, if the herd divided when they reached the clump of tamarisks?

But this operation had taken some time and when it was finished it was plainly too late for them to reach the forest.

Khamis judged the distance and said only three words: "Into the trees!"

There was only the one chance: to clamber up the branches of the tamarisks so as to avoid at least the first shock.

But first Max Huber and John Cort went into the wagon to load themselves with all the remaining packets of cartridges so as to ensure the use of the carbines; these would be necessary not only to open fire on the elephants but also for the return journey. This task was accomplished in a moment with the help of the Portuguese and the foreloper, who remembered to equip himself with his axe and flask. As they crossed the lower parts of the Oubanghi, who could tell whether he and his companions would succeed in reaching the factories on the coast?

What time was it now? . . . Seventeen minutes past eleven, as John Cort realised after consulting his watch by the light of a match. He had not lost the coolness which enabled him to sum up the situation: in his opinion it was one of great peril. If the elephants were to stop at the hillock, instead of going on eastward or westwards over the plain, there could be no escape.

Though more nervous, Max Huber realised the danger no less; he went to and fro near the wagon watching the great moving mass which now appeared ever more menacing against the distant sky. "It's artillery we should want!" he murmured.

Khamis did not let his feelings be seen. He had that amazing calmness of the African of Arab blood, a blood

THE VILLAGE IN THE TREETOPS

thicker than that of the white man, which blunts the feelings and is less perceptible of physical pain. Two revolvers in his belt, his rifle ready to be raised to his shoulder, he waited.

The Portuguese could not hide his despair, he thought rather of the irreparable loss of which he was the victim than of his own peril. He groaned, he protested, he gave vent to the most resounding oaths in his mother-tongue.

Llanga kept beside John Cort and watched Max Huber. He showed no signs of nervousness, for so long as his two friends were with him he felt no fear.

And yet the deafening uproar was increasing with unheard-of violence as that formidable cavalcade came nearer and nearer. The trumpeting of those mighty jaws redoubled. Already a blast could be felt traversing the air like the onset of a gale. Only four or five hundred paces away, the elephants seemed in the darkness immeasurably large, and of preternatural aspect. They might have been thought of as an apocalypse of monsters, whose trunks, like a thousand serpents, were writhing in frenzied agitation.

There was barely time to take refuge among the branches of the tamarisks, beneath which the herd might pass without noticing the Portuguese and his companions.

The trees, about sixty feet high, were so close together that their lower branches were interlaced, so that it should be possible to scramble from one to the next. Their trunks were about six to eight feet round at the base, and four to five feet at the fork. Would such thickness be strong enough if the animals were to charge up the mound?

The tree-trunks offered nothing but a smooth surface up to where their lowest branches jutted out some thirty feet from the ground, and so thick were they that to climb them would not have been easy if Khamis had not had several sjamboks at his disposal. These are thongs of rhinoceros hide, very supple, with which the forelopers control the bullock-teams.

Thanks to these thongs, Urdax and Khamis, after throwing them over a fork, were able to climb into one of the trees, and Max Huber and John Cort climbed into another.

As soon as they were astride of a branch, they lowered the end of the sjambok to Llanga, whom they hauled up by main force.

The herd was only about three hundred yards away, and in a few moments it would have reached the mound.

"Well, my friend, are you satisfied now?" John Cort asked his friend ironically.

"So far, John, it's only something unforeseen!"

"No doubt, Max, but one thing will be extraordinary, and that's if we can get safe and sound out of this business!"

"Yes . . . all things considered, John, it would have been better if we hadn't been exposed to this attack by elephants whose impact can sometimes be so brutal . . ."

"It's quite incredible, my dear Max, how completely we agree!" John Cort was content to reply.

What Max Huber said in answer his friend was unable to hear. At that moment there arose screams of fear, and then of agony, which would have made the bravest quail.

Thrusting aside the leaves, Urdax and Khamis could see what was happening a hundred or so paces away.

After making their escape, the cattle could flee only towards the forest. But these animals, with their slow measured pace, could they reach it before they were attacked? No, and they were quickly driven back. In vain they tried to defend themselves with kicks and thrusts of their horns. Of all the team there remained only one solitary animal; and this, unfortunately, sought to take refuge under the branches of the tamarisks.

Unfortunately indeed, for the elephants pursued it and then, by a common impulse, they stopped. In a few

THE VILLAGE IN THE TREETOPS

seconds the bullock was nothing but a mass of tattered flesh, of broken bones, of bloody fragments, trampled under the calloused feet with their nails as hard as iron.

Thus the mound was hemmed in, and all hope of seeing the furious beasts move off had to be given up.

In a moment the wagon was charged, overthrown, capsized, crushed beneath the heavy bodies which came blundering up the mound. Smashed like a child's toy, there remained nothing either of its wheels or of its body.

Doubtless fresh oaths were bursting from the lips of the Portuguese, but they did not suffice to stop these hundreds of elephants any more than the shot which he fired at the nearest, whose trunk was already encircling the tree he was on. The bullet rebounded from the animal's back without piercing its flesh.

Max Huber and John Cort fully realised this. Granting that not one of their shots were to miss, that every bullet found its billet, they might possibly have been able to free themselves from these terrible assailants, and to destroy them to the very last—if there had been only a few of them. Then the daylight would have disclosed nothing but a pile of enormous carcasses at the foot of the trees! ...

But three hundred, five hundred, a thousand of these animals! ... Is it indeed so rarely that such numbers are met with in equatorial Africa? Do not the travellers, the traders, speak of immense plains, covered with ruminants of every species so far as the eye can reach?

"This is getting rather involved ..." commented John Cort.

"You could almost say it's getting complicated!" Max Huber corrected him. Then, turning towards the small boy who was straddling the branch beside him. "You're not scared?" he asked.

"No, my friend Max ... with you ... no!" Llanga replied.

Yet it would have been legitimate, not only for the

child but even for grown men, to feel the heart overcome by irresistible fright.

There was indeed no doubt that the elephants would catch sight, between the branches of the trees, of all that remained of the caravan's personnel.

And then, as the more distant ranks thrust on the nearer, the circle around the mound began to contract. A dozen or so of the beasts, rearing upon their hind legs, were trying to reach the lower branches with their trunks. Fortunately, at that height of thirty feet they could not succeed.

Four carbine-shots rang out at once—four shots fired into the brown, for it was impossible to take aim through the dark foliage of the trees.

Cries even more violent, roars even more furious, could not be heard. But it did not seem that any of the elephants had been mortally wounded. And even if they had, all four of them, that would not have counted for much!

It was no longer with the branches that the trunks were trying to grapple, they surrounded the tree-boles, which were already sustaining the powerful thrust of the bodies. And, indeed, thick though these tamarisks were at their base, solidly though their roots were embedded in the soil, they would experience a shaking which no doubt they would be unable to resist.

Shots rang out again—only two this time—fired by the Portuguese and the foreloper, whose tree, shaken with extraordinary violence, threatened them with its immediate downfall.

The Frenchman and his comrade had not fired, ready though they were to do so.

"What's the good? ..." John Cort had said.

"Yes, we must reserve our ammunition," Max Huber replied. "Later we might regret having burned out our last cartridge here!"

While they were waiting, the tamarisk to which Urdax

THE VILLAGE IN THE TREETOPS

and Khamis were clinging was so weakened that it could be heard cracking all down its length.

Plainly it was not being uprooted, it was breaking. The beasts were attacking it with blows from their tusks, were bending it with their trunks, were shaking it right down to its roots. To stay any longer in that tree, even for a minute, was to risk being hurled to the ground.

"Come on!" the foreloper cried to Urdax, as he strove to reach the next tree.

But the Portuguese had lost his head, and was uselessly opening fire with his carbine and his revolvers, whose bullets were glancing off the tough hides of the elephants as though from an alligator's scales.

"Come on! . . ." Khamis repeated.

Then, at the very moment when the tamarisk was being shaken more violently than ever, he succeeded in grasping one of the branches of the tree occupied by the three others. Though the animals were still attacking it, it was less endangered than his own.

"Urdax?" asked John Cort.

"He wouldn't follow me," the foreloper replied. "He didn't know what he was doing."

"The poor wretch is going to fall!"

"We can't leave him there! . . ." protested Max Huber.

"We must get him in spite of himself . . ." John Cort agreed.

"Too late!" exclaimed Khamis.

It was indeed too late; snapped with a final cracking, the tamarisk fell to the ground.

What became of the Portuguese his comrades were unable to see. Cries showed that he was struggling beneath the feet of the elephants, then, as they stopped almost at once, that all was over.

"The poor wretch . . . the poor wretch!" murmured John Cort.

"Our turn soon . . ." said Khamis.

"That would be a pity!" was Max Huber's calm reply.

"Once more I quite agree with you, my friend," John Cort declared.

What could be done? . . . The elephants, trampling the earth, were shaking the other trees, which were swaying as though in a gale. The horrible end of Urdax—was it not also reserved for those who had survived him only by a few minutes? . . . Did they see any chance of getting clear of the tamarisk before it fell? . . .

And, if they risked climbing down to the plain, could they escape from the herd's pursuit? . . . Would they have time to reach the forest? . . . And, indeed, could this offer them any safety? . . . If the elephants did not pursue them, would they not have escaped only to fall into the power of natives no less fierce?

Nonetheless, if there were a chance of taking refuge beyond the edge of the forest, it must be seized without hesitation. It was only commonsense to prefer an uncertain peril to a certain one.

The tree kept on swaying, and this brought its lower branches within reach of the animal's trunk. So violent did its shaking become that the foreloper and his companions were on the point of letting go. Alarmed for Llanga, Max Huber flung his left arm around him while he held on with his right. Within a few moments either the roots would give way or the tree-trunk would snap at its base, and its fall would be the death of those who had sought refuge in its branches, the same frightful crushing as that of the Portuguese Urdax!

Under the strongest and most frequent of the thrusts, the roots at last gave way, the soil dropped clear and the tree subsided rather than fell on to the mound.

"The forest! . . . make for the forest!" shouted Khamis.

On the side where the tree branches had touched the ground, the elephants had recoiled, leaving the way clear. The foreloper, whose voice had just been heard, was at once on the ground and the three others followed him in his flight.

At first the animals, still attacking the rest of the trees,

THE VILLAGE IN THE TREETOPS

failed to notice the fugitives. With Llanga in his arms, Max Huber ran as fast as his strength would allow him. John Cort kept at his side, ready either to share that burden with him, or to open fire on the first of the animals that got within range.

They had hardly got a quarter of a mile away when about ten of the elephants, leaving the herd, began to hunt them.

"Courage! . . . Courage! . . ." cried Khamis, "keep on going . . . we'll get there!"

Yes, maybe, but it was essential not to be delayed. Llanga realised that Max Huber was tiring.

"Put me down! . . . put me down, my friend Max, I've got good legs . . . put me down!"

Max Huber did not listen, but simply tried not to get left behind. Half a mile was crossed without the animals' having made any perceptible gain. Then, unfortunately, the speed of Khamis and his friends began to slacken; that terrible rush had robbed them of their breath.

But the edge of the forest was only a few hundred paces off, and would not there be probable, if not certain, safety behind these dense masses in the midst of which the enormous animals would not be able to move? . . .

"Quick! . . . quick! . . ." Khamis repeated. "Give Llanga to me Mr. Max."

"No, Khamis . . . I'll go on to the end."

One of the elephants could be seen only about fifteen yards away; the blaring of its trunk could be heard, the warmth of its breath could be felt. The earth was trembling under the blows of its great galloping feet. Another minute and it would have reached Max Huber, who by now could hardly keep up with the others.

But John Cort halted, turned round, raised his carbine to his shoulder, took aim and fired: and it was clear that he had hit the elephant in the right place. The bullet had reached its heart and it dropped as though struck by lightning.

"Lucky shot!" he murmured, as he continued his flight.

The rest of the animals, when they came up a few seconds later, had to swerve to avoid this great heap sprawling on the ground. This gave the foreloper and his comrades a chance of which they had to take advantage.

Certainly after having torn down the rest of the trees the herd had not waited before dashing towards the forest.

Here no fires reappeared, neither at ground level, nor among the treetops. Everything seemed to blend into the outline of the dark horizon.

Weary and out of breath, would the fugitives have the strength to reach their goal?

"Come on! ... Come on! ..." cried Khamis.

If they had only fifty yards to cross, the elephants were only forty yards behind ...

By a supreme effort—the instinct of self-preservation —the three men threw themselves between the first of the trees and fell half dead upon the ground.

In vain the herd tried to get across the barrier. So tightly packed were the trees that the animals could not force a way between them, and so large were they that they could not break them down. In vain the trunks writhed between them, in vain those at the rear thrust against those in front.

The fugitives had nothing more to fear from the elephants, to whom the great Oubanghi forest opposed an insurmountable obstacle.

CHAPTER IV

DECISION TO MAKE, DECISION MADE

IT WAS nearly midnight and there were still six hours to be spent in complete darkness. Six long hours of peril and fear! . . . That Khamis and his comrades were sheltered behind the impassable barrier of trees, that was all to the good. But if their security were assured on that side, another danger menaced them. In the middle of the night had not these countless flames shown themselves on the edge of the forest? . . . Had not the treetops been lit up by an inexplicable gleam? . . . Could they doubt that a horde of natives were encamped somewhere in the vicinity? . . . Was not an attack to be feared? . . .

"Let's keep on the lookout," said the foreloper, as soon as he had regained breath after that exhausting run and his two comrades were in a condition to reply.

"Let's keep on the lookout," repeated John Cort, "and let's be ready to repulse an attack . . . The natives can't be far away . . . it was on this part of the forest-edge that they were camping, and look, here's the remains of a fire that's not quite gone out."

And indeed, at the foot of a tree five or six yards away, some cinders were still emitting a reddish glow.

Max Huber got up and, loading his carbine, went off into the undergrowth, while Khamis and John Cort anxiously waited ready to join him should it become necessary.

His absence only lasted three or four minutes. He had heard nothing suspicious, nor seen anything likely to make him fear an attack. "This portion of the forest is deserted now," he said, "the natives have certainly left it."

"Perhaps they fled when they saw those elephants coming," John Cort suggested.

"Perhaps, for those fires that we saw," said Khamis, "they went out as soon as they heard that roaring towards the north. Was that through prudence or simply through fear? Those fellows must certainly have felt themselves safe behind the trees.... I can't understand it at all...."

"It's quite inexplicable," replied Max Huber, "and the night doesn't favour looking for an explanation. Let's wait for daybreak, and I must say I'm having some difficulty in keeping awake ... in spite of myself my eyes are closing."

"It's a bad time to choose for a nap, my dear Max," John Cort reminded him.

"It couldn't be worse, my dear John, but sleep doesn't obey, it commands ... goodnight until tomorrow!"

In an instant Max Huber, stretched out at the foot of the tree, had fallen into a deep sleep.

"Go and lie down beside him, Llanga," said John Cort, "Khamis and I, we'll stay on guard till dawn."

"I'll be enough for that, Mr. John," the foreloper assured him, "I'm used to it, and I advise you to follow your friend's example."

They could trust themselves to Khamis. He would not relax his watch for a moment.

Llanga curled up near Max Huber. John Cort tried to hold out, and for another quarter of an hour he chatted with the foreloper. They discussed the unfortunate Portuguese, to whom Khamis had long been attached and whose good qualities they had learned to appreciate during that journey.

"The poor fellow," Khamis repeated, "he lost his head when he saw himself forsaken by those cowards of porters, robbed and stripped of all he possessed ..."

THE VILLAGE IN THE TREETOPS

"Poor man!" John Cort murmured. These were his last words. Overcome by weariness, he stretched himself out on the grass and fell asleep at once.

Alone, eyes and ears on the alert, listening for the slightest sound, his carbine within reach of his hand, staring into the thick darkness, occasionally getting up to investigate the depths of the undergrowth, ready to arouse his companion if they had to defend themselves, Khamis watched until the first gleams of day.

It is easy to realise the differences of character between the two friends.

John Cort had a very serious and very practical mind —qualities usual among the people of New England. Born in Boston, although he was a Yankee by birth he showed only the better qualities of the Yankee. Deeply interested as he was in geography, anthropology, the study of the races of mankind, most attracted his attention. To these merits he added a high courage, and he would have carried his devotion to his friends to the last sacrifice.

Max Huber, still a Parisian in the midst of these distant lands where the chances of life had taken him, yielded to John Cort neither in his head nor in his heart. He was less practical and he, so to speak, "lived in poetry," while his friend "lived in prose." His temperament led him to seek anything that was out of the ordinary, and he would have been capable of regrettable rashness to satisfy his imaginative instincts had not his prudent companions restrained him. This had happened more than once since they had left Libreville.

It was here that the two had met five or six years earlier, and they were united in a solid friendship. Their families owned considerable interests in an American factory near the town, and this enabled the two young men to devote themselves to more attractive occupations.

Three months previously they had formed a plan of visiting the region which stretches eastward from the

French Congo and the Cameroons. Determined hunters, they had not hesitated to join a caravan which was on the point of leaving the town for that region, abounding in elephants, beyond the Behar-el-Abiad. They both knew its leader, a native of Loango and rightly regarded as a very capable trader.

Urdax belonged to that Association of Ivory Hunters which Stanley had met when he was coming back from the northern Congo. But he did not share the bad reputation of his colleagues, most of whom, on the pretext of hunting the elephant, devote themselves to the massacre of the natives, so that, as that daring explorer of equatorial Africa said, the ivory that they collect is stained with human blood.

No, a Frenchman and an American could, without shame, accept the company of Urdax as well as that of the foreloper who acted as guide to the caravan, this Khamis who never in any circumstances swerved from his devotion and his zeal.

The journey had so far been fortunate. Quite habituated to the country, John Cort and Max Huber bore with remarkable endurance the fatigues of the expedition. Somewhat thinner, no doubt, they were returning in perfect health when ill-fortune barred their way. Now they had lost their leader and over a thousand miles still separated them from Libreville.

The "Great Forest," as Urdax had called it, this Oubanghi Forest, whose verge they had crossed, fully justified its name. Here, indeed, began that immense stretch of unknown country which extends parallel to the equator to the north of the Congo and is twice the size of France.

It had never entered the head of Urdax to venture through that forest; he meant to skirt it by the north and west. How indeed could the wagon and its team have been able to penetrate into the heart of that maze? Although it would increase their journey by several days' march, the caravan would follow the edge of the

THE VILLAGE IN THE TREETOPS

forest along an easier route which would lead to the right bank of the Oubanghi. Thence it would be easy to reach the factories at Libreville.

But now the situation was different. No longer the impedimenta of a large personnel with loads of cumbersome material. No wagon, no cattle, no camp-gear. Only three men and a boy, completely devoid of any means of transport and five hundred leagues from the Atlantic coast.

What ought they to do? Return to the route which Urdax had meant to follow, but under singularly unfavourable conditions . . . Try, on foot, to cross the forest obliquely, where contact with the natives would be less to be feared—a route which would shorten their journey to the borders of the French Congo? . . .

This was the important question, first to set out and then to decide, as soon as Max Huber and John Cort awoke at dawn.

For long hours Khamis stayed on guard. No incident disturbed the rest of the sleepers nor led him to fear any nocturnal attack. Several times, revolver in hand, he had gone about fifty yards away, crawling through the undergrowth whenever he heard any sound which made him feel uneasy. But it was only the crackling of dead branches, the wing-beats of some great bird, the tramp of some animal near the place where they were resting, or those vague sounds of the forest when the night winds disturb the treetops.

As soon as the two friends opened their eyes they were on their feet.

"What about the natives?" John Cort asked.

"I haven't seen anything of them," Khamis assured him.

"Haven't they left any signs that they were here?"

"That's to be supposed, Mr. John, probably near the edge of the forest . . ."

"Let's go and see, Khamis."

Followed by Llanga, the three went towards the plain.

Thirty paces away there was no lack of sign; countless footprints, grass crushed at the base of the trees, the remains of half-burnt resinous branches, piles of cinders, in which a few sparks were still crackling, ashes which still emitted a little smoke. But no human being beneath the trees or on those branches, among which, five or six hours, earlier, they had seen those moving flames.

"They've gone," Max Huber decided.

"Yes," agreed Khamis, "and it doesn't seem to me that we've anything to fear."

"If the natives have gone," John Cort pointed out, "the elephants haven't followed their example."

And indeed the monstrous beasts were still roaming about near the edge of the forest. Some of them were frantically trying, though in vain, to tear down the trees by vigorous thrusts. As for the clump of tamarisks, it was obvious that it had been torn down. Deprived of their shadows, the hillock formed only a mound on the plain.

At the foreloper's suggestion, Max Huber and John Cort took care not to show themselves: they hoped that the elephants would leave the district.

"That would let us go back to the camp," said Huber, "and collect what's left of our gear. . . . Perhaps a few boxes of preserved food or ammunition. . . ."

"And also," John Cort added, "to give poor Urdax proper burial . . ."

"We can't dream of that so long as the elephants are there," replied Khamis, "what's more, as for the rest of our gear it must have been reduced to shapeless fragments!"

The foreloper was right, and, as the elephants showed no signs of going away, all that remained to decide was what was best to do. So the four went back into the forest.

On their way Max Huber was lucky enough to kill a fine animal which would provide them with food for two or three days. It was an inyala, a sort of large ante-

THE VILLAGE IN THE TREETOPS

lope. The bullet had struck it as soon as its head had emerged from the thickets.

This animal must have weighed two hundred and fifty to three hundred pounds, and as soon as he saw it fall, Llanga had run towards it like a little dog. But naturally he could not carry such a load, and his friends had to go and help him.

The foreloper, who was used to this work, cut it to pieces and selected the eatable portions, which were brought back to the dying fire. John Cort threw on an armful of dead wood, which was soon ablaze; then as soon as a layer of glowing cinders had been formed, Khamis placed upon it several slices of appetising flesh.

Of the preserved food and the biscuits which the caravan had possessed, there was no longer any question; the porters had no doubt carried away most of them. Fortunately, in the game-rich forests of Central Africa, a hunter is always sure of providing for himself so long as he can make do on roast or grilled meat.

The most important thing was that there should be no lack of ammunition, for each of the men was equipped with a very accurate carbine and a revolver. Properly used, these weapons would be of good service to them, but they would still need the cartridge belts to be filled. But when they counted up, and although before leaving the wagon they had stuffed their pockets full, the men only had about fifty shots to fire.

A very inadequate supply, it must be admitted, especially if they should have to defend themselves against the wild beasts or the natives for the four hundred miles between themselves and the right bank of the Oubanghi. Beyond that point they would be able to obtain supplies without too much trouble; either in the villages or in the missionary settlements or even on the boats which go down that great tributary of the Congo.

After having stuffed themselves on inyala meat and refreshed themselves with the clear water of a rivulet which trickled between the trees, the three men discussed what they had better do.

John Cort began by saying, "Khamis, so far Urdax has been our leader. He always found us ready to follow his advice because we had confidence in him.... You have inspired us with the same confidence by your character and your experience ... Tell us what you think best to do in our present position, and you can be perfectly certain we'll agree."

"Certainly," Max Huber added, "we're not going to quarrel."

"You know this country, Khamis," John Cort continued, "for a number of years you've led the caravans with a devotion that we can well appreciate.... It is to your devotion and to your faithfulness that we appeal, and I know that neither the one nor the other will fail us...."

"Mr. John, Mr. Max, you can rely upon me," was the foreloper's simple reply. He shook the hands which were held out to him, and among which was that of Llanga.

"What's your advice?" John Cort asked him, "should we or should we not give up Urdax' scheme for skirting the forest on the west?"

"We've got to go through it," the foreloper replied unhesitatingly, "there we shouldn't encounter anything we don't want to. Wild beasts perhaps, but natives, no; none of these people ever risk themselves in the interior. The dangers would be greater for us in the plains, especially from the nomads. In that forest, where the caravan could never have gone, men on foot may be able to find their way. So I say again let's make for the southwest, and I've got a good hope of taking you without any difficulty to the Zongo rapids."

These rapids bar the course of the Oubanghi where it turns from the west towards the south; according to the travellers' reports, this marks the furthest point of the forest. Then all they would have to do would be to follow the plains parallel to the equator; and thanks to the caravans which are so numerous in that region they

THE VILLAGE IN THE TREETOPS

would have plenty of opportunity of getting food and transport.

Khamis' advice was good; moreover the route that he followed ought to shorten the distance to the Oubanghi. The only question was regarding the kind of obstacle which they might meet in the depths of the forest. They could not hope for any practicable footpath, only perhaps a few trails made by the animals. The ground was bound to be encumbered with undergrowth which really needed an axe, while the foreloper was reduced to a small hatchet and his companions to their knives. Nevertheless they ought not to encounter long delays during their journey.

After having answered these objections John Cort no longer hesitated. As to the difficulty of finding their direction under trees whose thick dome was hardly penetrated by the sun even at its highest point, there was no need to worry about it.

Indeed, a sort of instinct, like that of the animals—an inexplicable instinct found among certain races such as the savage tribes of the Far West—would enable them to guide themselves by hearing and scent rather than by sight. Khamis possessed this sense of direction to a very rare degree; he had often given clear proof of this. The others could trust to that aptitude, physical rather than intellectual and little subject to error, without needing to check their bearings by the sun. As to any other obstacles which the forest might offer, the foreloper replied:

"Mr. John, I know that we shan't find any footpaths across a soil obstructed with bushes, dead wood, and trees fallen with old age, but such obstacles are easy to cross. But can you imagine that so great a forest isn't watered by streams, which can only be the tributaries of the Oubanghi?"

"Even if it was only that which flowed not far from the hillock," Max Huber commented, "it was making for the forest and why shouldn't it become a river? . . . In that case a raft which we could construct . . . a few tree-trunks tied together . . ."

"Don't go so fast, my friend," John Cort told him, "and don't let your imagination carry you off down that rio . . . which is quite imaginary. . . ."

"Mr. Max is right," Khamis declared, "towards the setting sun we shall find some stream which must flow into the Oubanghi . . ."

"I quite agree," John Cort replied, "but, as we know, these African rivers are mostly unnavigable. . . ."

"You can see nothing but difficulties, my dear John . . ."

"Better see them before than after, my dear Max!"

John Cort had spoken the truth. The rivers of Africa do not offer the same advantages as do those of the rest of the world. Although they drain a considerable area, they do not much facilitate expeditions into the interior. The volume of their waters is much less abundant, and though their length equals that of other rivers they cannot carry ships even of medium tonnage very far from their mouths. What is more, there are shallows which intercept them, cataracts and waterfalls which extend from one bank to the other, rapids so violent that no vessel will dare to traverse them. This is one of the reasons why Central Africa has shown itself so difficult to explore.

So John Cort's objection was not without weight, and Khamis could not deny this. Yet it was not of a kind to call for the rejection of his scheme, which, on other grounds, offered real advantages.

"If we should meet a stream," he replied, "we'll go down it until we meet with any obstacles . . . if it's possible to go round them, we'll go round them. If not, we'll start walking again."

"So," John Cort replied, "I won't oppose your suggestion, Khamis, and I think that we shall do best to make for the Oubanghi by following one of its tributaries—if we can."

THE VILLAGE IN THE TREETOPS

The discussion thus having been settled there were only two words to say:

"*En route!*" exclaimed Max Huber.

And his companions echoed them after him.

In his heart, this scheme suited him; to venture into the interior of this immense forest, so far never penetrated, if not impenetrable. . . . Perhaps, there he would find that "something extraordinary," which, for three months, he had not been able to find in the regions of the Upper Oubanghi!

CHAPTER V

THE FIRST DAY'S MARCH

It was a little after eight when the travellers set off towards the south-west.

At what distance would they find the water-course which they counted on following until it reached the Oubanghi? . . . None of them could say. And if it was that which had appeared to be flowing towards the forest, after skirting the mound where the tamarisks grew, might it not diverge eastwards without traversing it? . . . And, finally, suppose obstacles, reefs or rapids, encumbered its bed and made it unnavigable? . . . On the other hand, if this immense agglomeration of trees were devoid of footpaths or of routes opened by the animals through the undergrowth, how would men on foot succeed in cutting their way without either steel or fire? . . . Would they find this district, so much frequented by great beasts, with the ground cleared, the bushes trampled down, the lianas broken, the way flung open? . . .

Llanga, as lively as a ferret, ran on ahead, though

John Cort advised him not to go too far away. But when he was out of sight his piercing voice never stopped being heard: "This way . . . this way!" he shouted.

And the other three went towards him, following the tracks which he had just made.

When they had to find their direction through this maze, the foreloper's instinct came in useful. Sometimes too, through openings in the branches, they could get their bearings from the sun. Yet here the foliage was so thick that hardly a twilight prevailed beneath these thousands of trees. In bad weather, this would almost become darkness, and during the night all movement would be impossible.

So Khamis meant to make a halt from evening till morning, to choose some shelter at the foot of one of the trees in case of rain and not to light any fire except to cook the game killed during the day. Although the forest might not be much frequented by the natives—and they had found no trace of those which had camped on its edge—it would be better not to make their presence known by a flame. A few glowing embers covered by the ashes would be enough for cooking, and there was no reason to dread the cold at this season.

Indeed, the caravan had already had much to suffer from the heat while traversing these tropical plains, where the temperature often became excessive. Under the shadow of these trees the travellers would find less to endure, and conditions would be more favourable for the long painful journey they had to make. It goes without saying that during the night, still warmed by the heat of the day, they would, so long as the weather was fine, find no inconvenience in sleeping in the open air.

It was the rain which was most to be feared in a country where all the seasons are rainy. Yet for a week the sky had cleared at the new moon and as it seems to have some effect on the weather, they might be able to count on a fortnight which would not be troubled by the elements.

THE VILLAGE IN THE TREETOPS

In this part of the forest, which sloped gently down towards the banks of the Oubanghi, the ground was not marshy, as no doubt it would be further south. The firm soil was encarpeted by a tall coarse grass which made movement slow and difficult where the feet of the animals had not trampled it.

"Well," commented Max Huber, "it's a pity that our elephants didn't come this way! They would have broken the lianas, ripped away the bushes, flattened the path, trampled down the undergrowth ..."

"And us with it ..." John Cort replied.

"That's true," agreed the foreloper. "Let's be satisfied with what the rhinos and the buffalos have done. Where they've gone we'll be able to follow."

While Max Huber was cursing the dwarf bushes which bristled everywhere, John Cort never tired of admiring these flowery carpets. And what a variety of trees! With their great leaves alone the natives have been able to build huts for a halt of several days.

And from this foliage came a concert of cries and songs which lasted from morning to night. The songs came from myriads of beaks piping more shrilly than the boatswain's whistle on a warship. And who would not be deafened by this host of parrots, owls, flying squirrels and so forth, not to speak of the humming-birds which clustered like a swarm of bees between the tall branches!

The cries were those of a simian colony, a hullabaloo of baboons, chimpanzees, mandrils and gorillas, the largest and most fearsome of all the apes of Africa. So far however, these animals, numerous though they were, had not shown any hostility against Khamis and his companions, the first men, no doubt, which they had seen in the heart of this Central African forest. There was reason to believe, indeed, that no human beings had ever ventured among these trees, and so their simian population showed more curiosity than anger. In other parts of Africa conditions are very different, for there man has long made his appearance. Ivory hunters, as well as hordes of bandits, native or otherwise, no longer surprise the monkeys, who have long witnessed the ravages which these adventurers carry out and which cost so much human life.

After a first halt in the middle of the day, a second was made at six in the evening. Travelling had offered real difficulties through this inextricable network of lianas, and to cut or break them was a painful task. Nonetheless for much of the way there had been footpaths chiefly made by the buffalos, some of which could be seen behind the bushes.

These animals are to be dreaded, thanks to their immense strength, and whenever they attack hunters have to avoid their charge. To shoot them between the eyes, not too low, so that the blow would be mortal, that is the most certain way of killing them. Neither of the two sportsmen had had a chance to try their skill against them, for they always kept out of range. Indeed, as there was no lack so far of antelope flesh, they must take care to be sparing with their ammunition. No gunshot should be heard during their journey, unless it were a matter of self-defence or of providing their daily food.

It was on the edge of a small clearing, when evening came, that Khamis gave the signal to halt, at the foot of a tall tree. It was one of the African cotton-trees whose roots are like flying buttresses and beneath which the travellers could find shelter.

"Our beds ready made for us!" exclaimed Max Huber. "No elastic mattress but one made of cotton, and we're going to sample it!"

Fire having been kindled with Khamis' flint and steel and tinder, the meal was like breakfast and lunch. Unfortunately—and how could they not get resigned to it?—there was a complete lack of the biscuit which had replaced bread during their journey. They contented themselves with grilled meat, and this satisfied much of their appetite.

THE VILLAGE IN THE TREETOPS

When supper was over, before they stretched themselves out between the roots of the cotton-tree, John Cort said to the foreloper; "If I'm not mistaken, we've been marching all day towards the south-west..."

"All day," replied Khamis, "every time I've been able to see the sun I've checked our direction."

"And how many leagues do you think we've covered today?"

"Four or five, Mr. John, and if we can go on in the same way, in less than a month we'll have reached the banks of the Oubanghi."

"Well," John Cort continued. "But isn't it prudent to expect some bad luck?"

"And also some good luck," retorted Max Huber, "who knows that we won't find some water-course which we can descend without trouble...."

"So far it doesn't seem likely, my dear Max..."

"That's because we haven't gone far enough towards the west," Khamis declared, "and I shall be much surprised if tomorrow... or the day after..."

"Let's act as if we weren't going to find a river," John Cort replied, "all things considered, a journey of a month, so long as the difficulties aren't any more insurmountable than on our first day, isn't going to scare hunters so well Africanised as ourselves!"

"And still," added Max Huber, "I'm much afraid that this mysterious forest will be completely devoid of any mystery!"

"So much the better, Max!"

"So much the worse, John!—and now, Llanga, let's go to sleep...."

"Yes, my friend Max," replied the boy, whose eyes were closing with weariness after the fatigues of a long journey during which he had never once lagged behind. So they had to carry him between the roots of a cotton-tree and choose the best corner for him.

The foreloper had offered to stay on watch all night, but to this his comrades would not consent. So they relieved each other every three hours, although there seemed nothing suspicious anywhere near the clearing. But prudence warned them to be on their guard until sunrise.

It was Max Huber who took the first spell of duty, while John Cort and Khamis stretched themselves out on the white down that had fallen from the tree.

Huber, his loaded carbine within reach of his hand, leaned against one of the roots and gave himself up to the charm of this peaceful night. In the depths of the forest all the noise of the day had ceased and nothing could be heard except a sort of regular breathing, the respiration of the sleeping trees.

The rays of the moon, high in the heavens, shone through the gaps in the foliage and sprinkled the ground with silver zig-zags. Beyond the clearing the undergrowth was lit up by the moonbeams.

Always sensitive to the poetry of nature, Max Huber seemed to taste it, to breath it in, to be dreaming without falling asleep. Did it not seem to him that he was the only living creature in the heart of this world of vegetation? . . .

World of vegetation—that was what his imagination made of the great Oubanghi forest!

"And," he thought, "if anyone wants to penetrate into the last secrets of the globe, does he have to go to the ends of its axis to find its mysteries? . . . Why, at the cost of frightful dangers and with the certitude of meeting obstacles maybe insuperable, why attempt the conquest of the two poles? . . . What would it lead to? . . . The solution of a few problems of meteorology, of electricity, of terrestrial magnetism! . . . Is it worth while adding to the necrologies of the austral and boreal regions? . . .

"Wouldn't it be much more useful, and more remarkable, instead of ploughing the Arctic and Antarctic Oceans, to investigate the infinite areas of these forests and to conquer their fierce impenetrability? . . . Why,

THE VILLAGE IN THE TREETOPS

there are so many of them in America, in Asia, in Africa, and yet so far no pioneer has either thought of making them his field of discovery, or had the courage to throw himself into that unknown world? ... Nobody has so far torn from these trees the secret of their riddle, as the people of old did from the ancient oaks of Dodona? ... And were not the mythologists right to people these woods with satyrs, dryads, hamadryads and imaginary nymphs? ...

"Anyhow, to keep to the discoveries of modern science, can't one imagine in these immense forests the existence of unknown beings, fitted for auch a habitat? ... In the Druidic period did not Transalpine Gaul shelter half-savage peoples, Celts, Germans, Ligurians, hundreds of tribes, hundreds of towns and villages, with their own special customs, their individual manners, their native originality—all within those forests, whose boundaries even the all-powerful Romans did not succeed in crossing without great effort? ..."

Such were the dreams of Max Huber.

And indeed, in these regions of equatorial Africa, has not legend proclaimed the existence of beings somewhat inferior to humanity, of half-fabulous creatures? ... Is not this forest on the borders of the country of the Nyam-Nyam, these tailed men—who, however, do not possess any caudel appendage? ...

Did not Stanley meet in these regions pygmies only a yard high, yet perfectly formed, with a fine gleaming skin, with great deer-like eyes, whose existence the missionaries have reported, sheltered under the undergrowth or perched on the great trees, and who have a chief which they obey? ... Had he not gone through five villages, abandoned the previous evening by their Lilliputian population? ... Did he not find himself in the presence of tribes whose members hardly weighed eighty pounds? ...

And yet these tribes were no less intelligent, industrious, war-like, fearsome with their tiny weapons to animals and to men alike, and much dreaded by the peasants of the upper Nile? . . .

Thus carried away by his imagination, his longing for something extraordinary, Max Huber insisted on believing that the Oubanghi forest must contain such strange types, of which the enthnographers do not suspect the existence. . . .

Why not human beings with only one eye like the Cyclops of legend, or whose nose, stretched out like a trunk, would allow them to be classed, if not along with the elephants, at least as something of a similar type? . . .

Under the influence of these scientific but fantastic dreams, Max Huber rather forgot his duty as a sentinel.

An enemy might have approached without having been noticed in time for Khamis and John Cort to get on the defensive. . . .

A hand fell on his shoulder.

"Eh! . . . what? . . ." He jumped.

"It's me," his comrade told him, "so don't take me for a savage!—Nothing suspicious? . . ."

"Nothing. . . ."

"It's the time we agreed you should go to sleep, my dear Max. . . ."

"Right, but I shall be much surprised if the dreams which I'm going to have while I'm asleep are as good as those I had without sleeping!"

The first part of the night had not been disturbed. Nor was the rest of it when John Cort had relieved Max Huber and when Khamis had relieved John Cort.

CHAPTER VI

STILL TOWARDS THE SOUTH-WEST

ON THE morrow, 11th March, the travellers had quite recovered from their fatigues and were ready to brave those of their second day's journey.

Leaving the shade of the cotton-trees, they went round the clearing, saluted by the myriads of birds which filled space with deafening music and with organ-like sounds which would have aroused jealousy in the virtuosos of Italian music.

Before pushing ahead, it was obviously wise to have a meal. This consisted only of cold antelope, with water from a river which flowed away to the left and from which the foreloper filled his flask.

For the first part of their journey they went right ahead, beneath branches already traversed by the first rays of the sun, whose position they carefully observed. This part of the forest was evidently frequented by large beasts, for tracks were everywhere. And indeed during the morning the travellers saw a few buffaloes and even two rhinoceroses, which however kept their distance. As these were not in a mood to fight, there was no need to waste cartridges on them.

The travellers did not stop till towards noon, when they had covered a good eight miles.

During their journey John Cort had been able to bring down a pair of bustards. The flesh, greatly esteemed by the natives, aroused equal enthusiasm during the mid-day meal in an American and a Frenchman. But first Max Huber had said that he would like roast meat to be substituted for grilled.

JULES VERNE

"Nothing easier," the foreloper had replied.

And one of the bustards, plucked, drawn and spitted on a ramrod, having been roasted to a turn before a lively crackling fire, was eagerly wolfed down.

Then Khamis and his comrades met with conditions more painful than those of the previous day.

As they went down towards the south-west they found trails less frequent, and they had to hack their way through bushes as coarse as the lianas whose ropes had to be cut with a knife. A fairly heavy rain fell for several hours, but so dense was the foliage that the ground received only a few drops.

Still, in the middle of a clearing, Khamis was able to fill his flask, which was already almost empty and the travellers might congratulate themselves on this, for in vain had he looked for any trace of a rivulet in the grass. Hence, probably, the rarity of animals and of practicable footpaths. "This doesn't make the proximity of a water-course seem likely," John Cort pointed out, as they settled down for the evening halt.

Nevertheless the direction they had chosen ought not to be changed, and this with more reason as it would lead to the Oubanghi basin.

"All the same," Khamis suggested, "failing that water-course that we saw yesterday evening at the camp, mayn't we come across another in this direction?"

The night of the 11th March was spent not between the roots of a cotton-tree but at the foot of another tree in no way inferior in height.

Watch was kept as usual, and sleep was troubled only by the distant bellow of a few buffaloes and rhinoceroses. It was not to be feared that the roars of a lion would join in this nocturnal concert, for these fearsome beasts scarcely inhabit the forests of Central Africa.

If their roaring were not heard, it was the same with the snorts of the hippopotamus. This was regrettable, for the presence of these amphibious creatures would have indicated the vicinity of a water-course.

THE VILLAGE IN THE TREETOPS

Next day the travellers set out at daybreak in overcast weather. A shot from Max Huber's carbine brought down an antelope about the size of a donkey. Thus was food assured for several days, and Khamis busied himself with cutting it up, a task which took an hour. Then, with this load divided between them—Llanga insisted on carrying his share—they pushed on.

"Well," exclaimed John Cort, "we can buy meat cheaply here, as it only costs us one cartridge . . ."

"So long as one's skilfull . . ." the foreloper replied."

"And above all, so long as he's lucky," added Max Huber, more modest than most hunters.

But if Khamis and his comrades had been able to spare the powder and to economise on their lead, if they had used them only to kill their food, the day was not to end without their carbines having been used in defence.

For a good half mile, the foreloper had even thought that he would have to repulse the attack of a troop of monkeys. These accompanied them to right and left for a good distance, some jumping from tree to tree, others gambolling and crossing the bushes in prodigious bounds which would have aroused envy in the most agile of gymnasts. Here appeared different types of apes, tall in stature and of three colours, yellow like the Arabs, red like the Indians of the Far West, black like the Kaffirs, and as fearsome as certain wild animals.

Yet this escort, which had appeared after the midday meal, vanished about two hours later, while the travellers were following a fairly wide footpath which stretched on out of sight. If they had to congratulate themselves on the advantages of a route so easy to follow, they had to regret the possibility of meeting the animals which might frequent it.

These were two rhinoceroses whose roars could be heard a short distance off. Khamis could not mistake them, and he ordered his companions to stop. "Bad

JULES VERNE

beasts, these rhinos!" he said, gripping his rifle, which he had been carrying slung over his shoulder.

"Very bad," Max Huber replied, "but anyhow they're only vegetarians."

"Which have a hard life!" Khamis added.

"What ought we to do?" asked John Cort.

"Try to get by without being seen," Khamis advised them, "or at least to hide ourselves while these ill-disposed creatures go by . . . perhaps they won't see us? . . . Still, we must be ready to shoot if they do see us, or they'll trample us down."

The carbines were examined and the cartridges placed ready for rapid reloading. Then, leaving the footpath, the travellers disappeared behind the thick bushes which bordered it to the right.

Five minutes later, when the roars were getting louder, these monstrous creatures appeared. They were travelling rather fast, with their heads held high and their tails coiled up on their backs. They were about four yards in length; ears erect, legs short and crooked, their prominent snouts armed with one horn with which they can deal formidable blows. And so hard are their jaws that they can eat without harm cacti with sharp thorns as easily as donkeys eat thistles.

They suddenly came to a stop and Khamis and his comrades could not doubt that they had been tracked down.

One of the rhinos approached the bushes.

Max Huber got ready to shoot.

"Don't fire at the legs! . . . aim at the head!" the fore-loper shouted to him.

An explosion, then two, then three, rang out. The bullets scarcely penetrated the thick hides and were completely wasted.

The explosions neither scared nor checked the animals and they were getting ready to trample down the undergrowth.

It was clear that this tangle of bushes would be no

THE VILLAGE IN THE TREETOPS

obstacle for these powerful beasts, that everything would be crushed in a moment. After escaping the elephants of the plain would the travellers escape the rhinoceroses of the great forests? . . . Whether such animals use their nose as a trunk or have it armed with a horn, they are equally strong . . . and here there was not that line of trees which had stopped the elephants in full career. If the four tried to run away they would be pursued and soon they would be caught up with. The tangle of lianas would slow them up, while the rhinoceroses would crash through it like an avalanche.

Yet among the trees a gigantic baobab might offer them a refuge if they could succeed in climbing into its lower branches. This would be to repeat the manoeuvre they had carried out in the tamarisk trees, and certainly that had ended badly. Was there any hope of things turning out better here?

Maybe so, for the baobab was tall and stout enough to resist any attack the animals might make.

On the other hand its fork was about fifty feet above the ground, and its trunk, swelling out like a gourd, offered no cranny in which foot or hand might find support.

The foreloper had realised that he could never hope to reach that fork, and Max Huber and John Cort were waiting for him to decide what to do.

At that moment the bushes beside the pathway quivered and a great head emerged.

A fourth shot rang out.

John Cort was no luckier than Max Huber. The bullet, hardly penetrating the shoulder, merely evoked from the animal a howl more terrible than before; its anger was only increased by the pain. It did not recoil; on the other hand with a vigorous rush it dashed through the undergrowth, while the other rhinoceros, barely grazed by a bullet from Khamis, made ready to follow.

Neither of the three men had time to reload. As for trying to scatter in all directions, to escape into the forest, it was too late. The instinct of self-preservation urged the three of them, with Llanga, to seek refuge behind the trunk of the baobab, which measured no less than six yards in circumference.

But if the first animal were to go round the tree while the second joined him from the other side, how could they evade this double attack? . . .

"The devil!" exclaimed Max Huber.

"The Lord, you should say!" replied John Cort.

And certainly they would have to give up any hope of salvation if Providence did not come to their rescue.

With a shock of alarming violence, the baobab trembled right down to its roots as though it were being torn out of the ground.

The rhinoceros, carried along in its terrible rush, had suddenly come to a stop. In one place where there was a crevice in the bark of the tree, its horn, like a woodcutter's wedge, had been driven in a foot deep. In vain it made the most violent efforts to get itself free. Even when it reared back on its stunted legs it was unable to do so.

The other animal, which had been furiously trampling down the bushes, halted, and the fury of the two may well be imagined.

Khamis glanced round the tree to see what had happened: "Let's clear out . . . clear out!" he cried.

He was understood rather than heard.

Without asking for any explanation, the other three followed him through the tall grass. To their great surprise they were not pursued by the rhinoceroses, and it was only after five minutes of an exhausting run that, at a signal from the foreloper, they pulled up.

"Whatever's happened?" asked John Cort, as soon as he had got his breath back.

"The animal couldn't get its horn out of the tree-trunk," Khamis explained.

"Heavens!" exclaimed Max Huber, "that's the Milo of Crotona of the rhinoceroses!"

THE VILLAGE IN THE TREETOPS

"And it'll end up like the hero of the Olympic Games!" added John Cort.

Khamis, caring little about that famous athlete of old, contented himself with saying: "Well, here we are . . . safe and sound . . . but at the cost of four or five cartridges thrown away!"

"That's still more regrettable because that beast . . . you can eat it if what I hear is right," said Max Huber.

"Yes," Khamis agreed, "although it's flesh tastes strongly of musk . . . we'll leave the beast where it is . . ."

"To pull its horn off whenever he likes!" Max Huber finished the sentence for him.

It would not have been prudent to go back to the tree; the two animals were filling the forest with their roars. After a detour which brought them back to the footpath, the travellers pushed on. About six they stopped at the foot of a gigantic rock.

The following day brought no incident. The difficulties of the route did not increase, and about twenty miles were covered towards the south-west. But as for the water-course so impatiently demanded by Max Huber and so definitely promised by Khamis, it did not show itself.

That evening, after a meal chiefly furnished by the monotonous antelope steak, they abandoned themselves to rest. Unfortunately their ten hours' sleep was troubled by the flight of thousands of bats of all sizes, from which the camp was not freed until daybreak.

"Too many of those harpies, far too many!" exclaimed Max Huber when he got to his feet, still yawning after so bad a night.

"We mustn't complain," the foreloper told him.

"But why not?"

"Because it's better to deal with bats than mosquitoes and so far they've spared us."

"What would be best of all, Khamis, would be to avoid both of them."

"Mosquitoes . . . we won't be able to avoid them, Mr. Max."

"And when shall we be eaten alive by those abominable insects?"

"When we get near a rio."

"A rio!" exclaimed Max Huber. "But I've believed in that rio so much, Khamis, I can't believe in it any longer!"

"Then you're wrong, Mr. Max, and perhaps it isn't so far away!"

The foreloper had, in fact, noticed certain changes in the nature of the soil; and about three in the afternoon, his observations tended to be confirmed. This part of the forest was clearly becoming marshy, and here and there were puddles bristling with aquatic plants. The travellers could even bring down some wild ducks, whose presence indicated the proximity of a water-course. And, as the sun began to set, the croaking of frogs could be heard.

"Either I'm sadly mistaken . . . or the mosquito country isn't far away," the foreloper commented.

During the rest of the day progress was made over difficult country, hindered by innumerable plants whose development was favoured by the damp warm climate. The trees, more widely spaced, were less encumbered with lianas.

Max Huber and John Cort could not misunderstand the changes in that south-western part of the forest; but, in spite of Khamis' forecasts, they could not anywhere see the gleam of running water.

The steeper the slope of the ground became, the more numerous were the swamps, and the travellers had to take care not to be swallowed up in them. And even getting out of them could not be accomplished without their being stung.

Thousand of leeches were swarming in the water, and on its surface ran thousands of gigantic millipedes, whose blackish colour and red legs aroused an insurmountable disgust.

On the other hand, what a treat for the eyes were the countless butterflies with their gleaming colours and the graceful dragonflies!

THE VILLAGE IN THE TREETOPS

The foreloper pointed out that not only wasps but also Tsetse flies abounded in the undergrowth. Fortunately, if they had to avoid the stings of the former, the travellers had no need to worry about the bites of the latter. Their venom is mortal only to horses, camels and dogs, and not to man any more than to the wild beasts.

The travellers went on towards the south-west until half past six, a journey at once long and wearisome. Already Khamis was trying to find a good place to stop for the night, when Max Huber and John Cort were aroused by the cries of Llanga. The little boy had run ahead as usual, ferreting from side to side, and they could hear him shouting at the top of his voice. Was he in the grip of some wild animal? . . .

The two men rushed in his direction, ready to open fire . . . But they were quickly reassured.

Standing on an enormous fallen trunk, and stretching out his hand towards a great clearing, Llanga was repeating in his shrill voice:

"The rio! . . . The rio!"

Khamis came up to join them, and all that John Cort said to him was, "The water-course we were asking for."

About a quarter of a mile away, through a large treeless glade, a clear river was reflecting the last rays of the sun.

"It's there that we ought to camp, to my mind," suggested John Cort.

"Yes . . . there . . ." the foreloper agreed, "and you can be sure that that rio will take us down to the Oubanghi."

Indeed it would not be difficult to build a raft on which to entrust themselves to the river-current.

But before reaching its bank they had to cross some very marshy soil, and as twilight lasts only a very short time in the equatorial regions, darkness was already complete when the travellers arrived on a fairly high

JULES VERNE

bank. Here the trees were scattered, but upstream and down they formed larger clumps.

John Cort estimated the breadth of the river at something over forty yards. So it was not a mere stream but a tributary of a certain importance whose current did not seem to be too swift.

To wait till next day to decide what to do, that seemed best. The most urgent thing was to discover some shelter in which to pass the night, and Khamis was lucky enough to find a crevice in the rocks, where a sort of cave opened out in the limestone of the river bank, large enough to hold the four of them.

They decided first to eat the remains of the cold meat, so that they would not need to light a fire, whose gleam might attract the animals. Crocodiles and hippopotami abound in these African rivers, and if they frequented this river—which certainly seemed probable—it would be better for the travellers not to have to defend themselves against their nocturnal attack.

Certainly a fire kindled in the opening of the cave and emitting a cloud of smoke would have scattered a crowd of mosquitoes which swarmed at the foot of the bank. But of two nuisances it was better to choose the lesser and to brave the stings of the insects rather than the enormous jaws of the alligators.

For the first few hours, John Cort kept watch at the opening of the crevice. Meanwhile, in spite of the buzzing of the mosquitoes, his companions slept deeply.

During his watch, though he saw nothing suspicious, at least he thought he could more than once hear a word which seemed to be pronounced by human lips in plaintive tones . . . And that word, it was *ngora*, which means "Mother" in the native language.

CHAPTER VII

THE EMPTY CAGE

How COULD they fail to congratulate the foreloper on having so conveniently found this cave, formed by the natural structure of the bank? On the ground a fine dry sand; no trace of dampness, neither on the cave wall nor on the roof. Thanks to that shelter the travellers had suffered nothing from a heavy rain which did not stop until midnight, and they could stay in the same place as long as was necessary to build a raft.

A fairly strong wind was blowing from the north and clearing the sky for the first rays of the sun. Everything indicated a hot day, and perhaps the travellers might come to regret the shade of the trees under which they had been walking for the last five days.

John Cort and Max Huber did not try to conceal their delight. This river was going to carry them, without any effort on their part, for a journey of about 250 miles to its junction with the Oubanghi, of which it must form a tributary. Thus would have been accomplished the last three-quarters of the journey; this was worked out fairly accurately by John Cort from the information which the foreloper gave him.

They looked to right and left, to north and south.

Upstream the river, which was flowing almost straight, disappeared, about half a mile away, beneath the trees.

Downstream, the foliage thickened at a distance of only about five hundred yards, where the river turned sharply to the south-east. It was beyond this turning that the forest regained its normal thickness.

A large marshy clearing occupied this part of the right bank. On the opposite shore the trees were thickly crowded together: a dense forest covered the surface of an undulating country whose crests, lit by the rising sun, were standing out against the distant horizon.

In the river bed clear water was flowing quietly along, filling it completely and sweeping down old tree-trunks and masses of grass torn away where the banks were erroded by the current.

John Cort then recalled that he had heard the word *ngora* uttered near the cave during the night, so he tried to see whether any human creature were prowling about in the vicinity.

That some nomads might have ventured down this river to reach the Oubanghi, that was certainly possible. Hence there was no need to assume that this immense area of the forest was either frequented by wandering tribes or inhabited by more settled communities.

He could see no human creature either on the edge of the marsh or on the banks of the river.

"I must have been the sport of a delusion," he thought, "it's just possible that I fell asleep for the moment and that I heard that word in my dreams." And so he said nothing of the incident to his companions.

"My dear Max," he asked, "Have you apologised to our good Khamis for having doubted the existence of this rio, which he never doubted himself?"

"He was quite right, John, and I'm very glad to have been wrong, for the current is going to take us quietly downstream as far as the Oubanghi."

"Quietly! I wouldn't say that," replied the foreloper. "There may be waterfalls or rapids."

"Let's only look on the good side of things," suggested John Cort, "we were looking for a river and here it is. We were thinking of building a raft, so let's build it."

"This very morning I'll set to work," Khamis told

THE VILLAGE IN THE TREETOPS

them. "And if you'll be good enough to help me, Mr. John..."

"Certainly, Khamis. And while we're working Max can go and look for some food."

"What makes that more urgent," Max Huber insisted, "is that there isn't anything left to eat. That glutton of a Llanga ate it all up yesterday evening."

"Me... my friend Max!" Llanga, who took this quite seriously, seemed deeply hurt by the accusation.

"Oh, my boy, you can see I was only joking!... Well, come with me. We'll follow the bank as far as the bend in the river. With the marsh on one side and running water on the other, there should be no lack of game either to right or left, and, who knows, maybe some fine fish to vary our menu."

"Look out for the crocodiles, Mr. Max, and even for the hippos," the foreloper advised them.

"Well, Khamis, a slice of roast hippopotamus is not to be despised, I fancy!... How could an animal with so pleasant a character—it's only a freshwater pig after all—fail to have nice tasty flesh?"

"A pleasant character, that's quite likely, Mr. Max, but when it's angry its wrath is terrible!"

"Still we ought to be able to cut a few pounds off him without making him angry...."

"Anyhow," added John Cort, "if you see the least sign of danger come back at once. Keep a sharp lookout."

"And you, you can keep calm, John—Come on, Llanga."

"Go along, my boy," John Cort told him, "and don't forget that we're entrusting your friend Max to you!"

After this advice, they could be quite certain that nothing untoward would happen to Max Huber, for Llanga was there to look after him.

Huber took his carbine and saw that his cartridge-belt was filled.

"Be careful of your ammunition, Mr. Max," the foreloper warned him.

"As much as I can, Khamis. But it's the greatest pity

that nature hasn't given us a cartridge-tree just as it's created the bread-fruit tree and the butter-tree in the African forest! Then as we went by we could gather cartridges just as we gather figs or dates!"

After making this comment, whose justice could not be denied, Max Huber went off with Llanga along a sort of footpath at the foot of the cliff. Soon they were out of sight.

John Cort and Khamis then went to look for wood suitable for building a raft. Even if this were to be only very crude they would have to get the material together.

All that they had was an axe and their knives. With such tools, how could they attack the giants of the forest or even their smaller companions? So Khamis decided to use fallen branches which he could tie together with the lianas and on which he would build a sort of decking of mixed earth and grass. About twelve feet long and eight feet wide, such a raft would be enough to carry three men and a boy who would be landing for meals and at night.

There was plenty of this wood on the marsh, brought down by the wind or by the lightning. By evening, Khamis promised, he would have collected everything he needed to build the raft. He told John Cort so and the latter said he was ready to go with him.

A last glance upstream and down having shown that everything near the marsh was quiet, the two set out.

They had only to go a hundred or so paces to find suitable material. The great difficulty would be to drag it to the water's edge, but if it were too heavy for two men to move they would have to wait for the hunters to return.

Meanwhile, everything went to show that Max Huber was having good hunting. An explosion had just rung out and the skill of the hunter was sufficient to ensure that his shot would not have been wasted. To be sure, with a sufficiency of ammunition, the travellers ought to be certain of their food during the 250 miles which

THE VILLAGE IN THE TREETOPS

separated them from the Oubanghi and even for a longer journey.

But while Khamis and John Cort were busy selecting the best pieces of wood their attention was attracted by shouts coming from the direction which Max Huber had taken.

"That's Max's voice!" exclaimed John Cort.

"Yes," agreed Khamis, "and Llanga's."

And indeed shrill cries were mingled with the masculine shouts.

"Are they in any danger?" John Cort wondered.

The two went back across the marsh and climbed to the top of the mound into which their cave opened. Thence, looking downstream, they could see Max Huber and the native boy standing on the bank. There were no other human beings or animals near them, and their gestures did not suggest any uneasiness but only indicated an invitation to join them.

When the two others had reached them, all that Max Huber said was, "Perhaps, Khamis, you won't have to trouble to build a raft."

"But why not?" the foreloper asked him.

"Here's one already made . . . in bad condition, it's true, but made of sound material."

And he showed them, by the side of the bank, a sort of platform, a collection of beams and planks, held together by a half-rotten cord whose end was tied to a stake driven into the ground.

"A raft!" John Cort exclaimed.

"Yes, it's certainly a raft!" agreed Khamis.

And indeed there could be no doubt as to the purpose of these beams and planks.

"Have natives come down the river as far as this?" Khamis wondered.

"Natives or explorers," John Cort replied, "and yet if this part of the Oubanghi forest had been explored, they would have heard about it in the Congo or the Cameroons."

"Anyhow," Max Huber pointed out, "that doesn't matter; the great thing is to know whether this raft—or what's left of it—can be useful to us."

"Yes, of course."

And the foreloper was about to go down to the water's edge when he was stopped by a shout from Llanga.

The boy, who had gone about fifty yards upstream, was running back to them and waving something in his hand.

In an instant he had handed that something to John Cort. It was an iron padlock, corroded by rust, bereft of its key, and its works obviously in no condition to act.

"Certainly," Max Huber pointed out, "it can't be a question of natives from the Congo or anywhere else, for they know nothing of the mysteries of the locksmith's art! . . . It must be white men whom the raft brought as far as this bend in the river!"

"And who have gone away and never come back!" added John Cort.

This was a reasonable deduction. The state of rust of the padlock, like the dilapidation of the raft, showed that several years must have elapsed since the one had been lost and the other abandoned on the bank of the creek. Two deductions followed from these indisputable facts. So when John Cort put them forward, Max Huber and Khamis had no hesitation in accepting them:

1. Some explorers or travellers, who were certainly not natives, had reached this clearing, after embarking either above or below the edge of the great forest.

2. The said explorers or travellers had for some reason or other left their raft at this point before going off to investigate that portion of the forest situated on the right bank.

Whatever the reason, none of them had ever come back. But neither John Cort nor Max Huber could remember that, since they had lived in the Congo, there had been any question of such an exploration.

If this was not extraordinary, it was at least unex-

THE VILLAGE IN THE TREETOPS

pected, and Max Huber had to relinquish the honour of being the first to visit this great forest, wrongly regarded as impenetrable.

Meanwhile, completely indifferent to this question of priority, Khamis was carefully examining the beams and planks of the raft. The former were in a fairly good condition, though the latter had suffered more from the weather, and three or four of them would have to be replaced. But anyhow there would be no need to build a completely new raft; a few repairs would be enough. The foreloper and his comrades, as surprised as they were pleased, now posessed the floating contrivance which would enable them to reach the place where the rio joined the main stream.

While Khamis was busying himself with this, the two friends exchanged ideas regarding the incident.

"There's no mistake about it," repeated John Cort, "some white men have already traversed the upper part of this river—white men, there's no doubt about that . . . That this raft, made of large pieces, might have been the work of the natives, agreed! . . . but there's the padlock. . . ."

"Yes, the padlock . . . not to mention any other article we might be able to pick up," commented Max Huber.

"Any other article, Max?"

"Well, John, it's quite possible that we might find the remains of a camp, though there's no trace of it in that cave where we spent the night. That might well have served as a place for a temporary halt, and I don't doubt that we weren't the first to seek refuge in it . . ."

"That would be evidence, my dear Max. Let's go as far as the bend in the rio . . ."

"Yes, John, it's there that the clearing ends and I shouldn't be surprised if a little further on . . ."

"Khamis?" exclaimed John Cort.

The foreloper came back to them.

"Well, what about that raft?" John Cort asked him.

"We can repair it without too much trouble, I'm going to collect all the wood we'll need."

"Before we start work," Max Huber suggested, "let's go down-stream along the bank. Who knows whether we shan't pick up some utensils bearing a trade-mark which would show their origin? That would be very useful to complete our cooking arrangements, which aren't at all adequate! . . . A flask, and not even a cup or a saucepan! . . ."

"You don't expect, my dear Max, to find a kitchen or a table where meals will be set out all ready for the passer-by?"

"I don't expect anything, my dear John, but we're in the presence of something inexplicable. Let's try to imagine some plausible explanation."

"Right, Max. There won't be anything inconvenient, Khamis, in our going about half a mile away?"

"So long as you don't go around the bend," the foreloper told them. "As we've got a method of going by water, let's spare ourselves a needless walk."

"Agreed, Khamis," John Cort replied. "And while the current is sweeping our raft along, we'll have plenty of leisure to see if there are any signs of a camp on either of the banks."

The three men and Llanga followed the bank, a sort of natural dyke between the marsh and the river. As they walked along they never stopped looking down, hoping to find footprints or some object left on the ground.

In spite of a careful examination, both on the top and at the foot of the bank, they found nothing. Nowhere were there any traces of anybody's going by or halting.

When Khamis and his comrades reached the first line of trees they were greeted by the cries of a troop of monkeys. These did not seem particularly surprised at the appearance of human beings, but nonetheless they made off.

"After all," John Cort pointed out, "it wasn't they who

THE VILLAGE IN THE TREETOPS

built the raft, and however intelligent they may be, they haven't yet taken to using padlocks..."

"Any more than cages, that I know of," Max Huber interrupted him.

"Than cages?" exclaimed John Cort, "what's the idea, Max, of talking about cages?"

"It's because I think I can see ... between the thickets ... about twenty yards from the river-bank ... some sort of construction...."

"Some ant-hill shaped like a hive; that's the sort the white ants of Africa build," John Cort replied.

"No, Mr. Max isn't wrong," Khamis declared. "Down there ... yes, it seems to be a sort of hut built at the foot of two of the mimosas and its front looks like trellis-work...."

"A cage or a hut," Max Huber replied, "let's see what's inside it...."

"Be careful," the foreloper reminded them, "and let's keep in the shelter of the trees."

"What's there to be afraid of?" As usual, Max Huber was spurred on both by curiosity and by impatience.

Anyhow, the neighbourhood seemed to be deserted. All that could be heard was the song of the birds and the cries of the monkeys as they dashed away. No trace, old or recent, of any camp appeared on the edge of the clearing. Nothing on the surface of the water, which was sweeping along great tufts of grass. On the other bank there was the same appearance of solitude and loneliness.

The last hundred yards were quickly made along the bank, which curved to follow the bend of the river. Here the marsh ended and the soil was getting drier as it rose beneath the dense undergrowth.

The strange construction could now be clearly seen, supported by the mimosas and covered by a sloping roof concealed beneath a thatch of yellowing grass. It showed no opening in its side, and the fallen lianas hid its walls right down to their base.

What made it look like a cage was the grille in its front wall, similar to that which, in the menageries, separates the wild beasts from the public.

That grille had a door—a door which now stood open. The cage itself was empty.

Max Huber, who was the first to rush inside, realised this at once.

Of utensils, there still remained a few, a saucepan in fairly good condition, a mug, a cup, three or four broken bottles, a woollen coverlet somewhat gnawed away, a few rags of material, a rusted axe, a spectacle-case, so rotten that the name of its manufacturer could no longer be read.

In one corner lay a copper box whose firmly-closed lid must have preserved its contents—provided that it did contain anything.

Max Huber picked it up and tried to open it but failed. Rust was making its two parts stick together. He had to slide his knife between the lid and it gave way.

The box contained a note-book in a good state of preservation. On the cover of this note-book were imprinted two words which he read aloud:

DR. JOHAUSEN

CHAPTER VIII

DR. JOHAUSEN

IF JOHN CORT, Max Huber and even Khamis had not burst into exclamation on hearing that name, it was because amazement had robbed them of speech. The very word "Johausen" was a revelation. It unveiled part of the mystery which covered the most fantastic of modern

THE VILLAGE IN THE TREETOPS

scientific experiments, in which comedy was mixed with the serious—and with tragedy too, for it seemed likely the attempt had led to the most deplorable results.

The efforts made by the American Professor Garner may still be remembered—his scheme for studying the language of the monkeys and of giving his theories experimental verification. The professor's name, the articles and books which he had published in America and Europe, could not have been forgotten by the people of Africa—especially by John Cort and Max Huber.

"Him at last," cried the former, "him whom we hadn't had any news of . . ."

"And whom we never shall have any news of, because he's no longer here to give it! . . ." exclaimed the latter.

"Him," for the Frenchman and the American, was Dr. Johausen. But, putting the doctor on one side for a moment, that is what had happened to Professor Garner. It was not this Yankee who could say what Rosseau said of himself at the beginning of his *Confessions*: "I am carrying out an enterprise which has had no exemplars and which will never have any imitators," for Professor Garner had had an imitator.

Before setting off for the Dark Continent, the Professor had got into touch with the world of monkeys—with the world of trained monkeys, that is. From his long and detailed studies of these animals he had gained the conviction that they could speak, that they could understand one another, that they could use an articulate language, that they used certain words to show that they wanted to drink. Within the Washington Zoo, Professor Garner had placed phonographs arranged to record the words of their vocabulary. He had even noticed that the monkeys—which is what distinguishes them from men—never speak unless they have to. He was led to express his opinion along these lines:

"The knowledge that I have of the animal world has given me the firm conviction that all the mammals are able to speak as much as one would expect, having regard to their experiences and their needs."

Even before Professor Garner had begun his studies, it was well known that such mammals as dogs and monkeys have their mouths and throats arranged somewhat on human lines and their glottis organised to emit articulate sounds. But it was known too—with due regard to the monkey-lovers—that thought came before speech. In order to speak it is necessary to think, and thinking demands the power of using general terms—a faculty which the animals lack. The parrot talks, but it does not understand a word of what it says.

The truth, in short, is that, if the animals do not talk, it is because nature has not given them enough intelligence, for there is nothing else to stop them. Indeed, as one scientist has pointed out, "for them to have a language they would need to have powers of judgment and of reasoning based, at least implicitly, on abstract and universal concepts." But though these rules are only common sense, Professor Garner thought but little of them.

There is no need to say that his theories were widely disputed. So he had determined to get into direct contact with their subjects, whom he would meet in large numbers and in great variety in the forests of tropical Africa. When he had learned gorilla-talk and chimpanzese he would return to America and publish a dictionary and grammar of the monkey language. Then everybody would be compelled to yield to the evidence and admit that he was right.

Had the professor kept the promise which he had made to himself and to the world of science? . . . That was the question and it was plain that Dr. Johausen did not believe it.

In 1892, Professor Garner had left America for the Congo. He had reached Libreville on 12th October, and taken up his home in one of the town's factories until February, 1894.

THE VILLAGE IN THE TREETOPS

It was only then that the Professor decided to begin his work. After having gone upstream in a small steamship, he landed at Lambaréne, and on 22nd April he arrived at the Catholic mission of Fernand-Vaz.

The Fathers of the Holy Spirit welcomed him and gave him hospitality in their house, built on the edge of the magnificent lake of the same name. The Doctor had nothing but praise for the care that the missionaries had given him and they had neglected nothing to facilitate his adventurous zoological experiment.

Just behind the mission there were grouped the first trees of a great forest abounding in monkeys, and no circumstances could be imagined more favourable for getting into touch with them. But what was needed was to live in intimate contact with them and, in short, to share their existence.

It was with this aim in view that Professor Garner had had made a portable iron cage, which he had taken into the forest. If he were to be believed, he had lived there three months, most of that time alone, and had been able to study the apes in their natural condition.

The truth is that the prudent American had simply erected his metallic house within twenty minutes' walk of the mission, and quite near to its spring, in a place to which he gave the name of "Fort Gorilla." He had even slept in it three consecutive nights. Devoured by the swarms of mosquitoes, he could not hold out any longer, so he had taken down his cage and asked from the Fathers of the Holy Spirit a hospitality which they readily gave him. At last, on 18th June, leaving the Mission for good, he had returned by way of England to America, taking as the only souvenir of his journey two tiny chimpanzees who obstinately refused to talk.

That was the result which Professor Garner had obtained. Indeed, it seemed only too certain that the dialect of the monkeys—if there were any such thing—was still to be discovered, like the basis on which their language is formed.

The Professor still maintained that he had picked up several vocal signs with a precise significance, *Whouw* for example, meaning "food;" *Cheny*, meaning "drink;" *Legk*, meaning "look out;" and there were several others which he had carefully noted down. Later, as a result of experiments made in the Washington Zoo, and thanks to the use of the phonograph, he declared that he had heard a generic word referring to everything having to do with food and drink; another for the use of the hands; and another for the computation of time.

In short, according to him, this language was composed of eight or nine principal sounds, varied by thirty or so modulations; he even gave their musical tones, which were almost always in *la* sharp.

Finally, and according to his opinion, in conformity with the Darwinian theory of the unity of species and the hereditary transmission of physical qualities and not of defects, it could be said, "If the human races are derived from an ape-like stem, why should not the human language be derived from the primitive speech of these anthropoids?" The only thing was, did man really have monkeys for his ancestors? . . . That was what remained to be shown and what has not yet been shown.

In short, the so-called language of the monkeys, detected by the naturalist Garner, was only a series of sounds which the mammals produce to communicate with their fellows, as indeed do all the animals, from dogs to ants. And, as one observer pointed out, such communications can be made not only by cries but by gestures or by special movements. If they do not express thoughts properly so-called, at least they express vivid impressions and feelings such as delight or terror.

So it was perfectly clear that the question had not been settled by the incomplete studies of the American Professor, which indeed, were practically devoid of experimental basis. And so two years later a German doctor hit on the idea of continuing the attempt by being transported, not merely twenty minutes from a mission,

THE VILLAGE IN THE TREETOPS

but right into the heart of the forest, into the midst of the world of monkeys. He would do so were he to be devoured alive by the mosquitoes, which Professor Garner's passion for the apes had not been able to withstand.

There then lived at Malinba in the Cameroons a certain scientist called Johausen. He had been there several years, and though he was a doctor he was more enthusiastic for biology than for medicine. As soon as he heard of the fruitless experiment of Professor Garner, he made up his mind to continue it, although he was over fifty years old. John Cort had had several discussions with him at Libreville.

If he were no longer young, Dr. Johausen at least enjoyed splendid health. Speaking English and French like his own mother tongue, thanks to carrying out his profession he also understood the native dialect. His wealth enabled him to give his services free of charge, for he had no relatives whatever. Independent in every sense of the word, not responsible to anyone, and filled with a confidence in himself which nothing could shake, why should he not do whatever he wished? It must be added however, that he had what is colloquially known as "a bee in his bonnet."

The doctor had in his service a native on whom he could rely. As soon as he heard of the scheme for going to live in the forest in the midst of the monkeys, this fellow had no hesitation in accepting his master's invitation to accompany him, although he did not realise too clearly what he was undertaking.

It was at this point that Dr. Johausen and his servant got to work. A portable cage, after the style of Garner's but better fitted up and more comfortable and made in Germany, was brought on a steamer which touched at Malinba. In that town they could easily get together so much food and ammunition that they would need no further supplies for some time.

As to their equipment, it was quite rudimentary; bedding, clothing, articles of toilet, cooking gear, as well as an old barrel-organ which the Doctor ordered with the idea that the monkeys might not be insensitive to the charms of music. He also had struck some medals bearing his name and portrait; these he meant to give to the rulers of the simian colony he hoped to found in Central Africa.

So at last, on 13th February, 1896, the Doctor and the native embarked at Malinba with their gear and went up the Nbarri river with the idea of going ...

Of going where? ... That was what Dr. Johausen had not said and what he refused to say to anyone. He would have no need of anything else, and the native and he would be sufficient for one another. He would have nothing to take his mind off the apes who would be his only society, and he would content himself with the delights of their conversation, never doubting that he would be able to unravel the secrets of their language.

What was known later was that his boat, having gone upstream for about a hundred leagues, had been moored off a village called Nghila, that a score of natives had been engaged as porters and that the gear had been carried off towards the east. But thenceforward nothing had been heard of Dr. Johausen. The porters, who had returned to the village, were unable to say exactly where they had left him.

In short, two years had elapsed and in spite of a few investigations which had led nowhere, there had been no news either of the German doctor or of his faithful servant.

But what had happened John Cort and Max Huber were able to work out—to a certain extent at any rate.

Dr. Johausen, with his escort, had reached a river in the north-west of the Oubanghi forest. There he had constructed a raft from the planks and beams he had brought with him. Then this work completed and his escort dismissed, his servant and he had gone down this unknown rio, and had stopped and erected their cabin where it had just been discovered under the trees on the

THE VILLAGE IN THE TREETOPS

right bank of the stream. This was all that appeared certain, but what theories could be framed regarding his present position! . . .

Why was the cage empty? . . . Why had its two inmates left it? . . . How many months, how many weeks, how many days, had they stayed in it? . . . Had they gone away of their own free will? That hardly seemed likely . . . So had they been carried off? . . . But by whom? . . . By the natives? . . . But the Oubanghi forest was supposed to be uninhabited . . . Was it likely that they had been attacked by wild beasts? . . . Finally, were the Doctor and the native still alive? . . .

These questions were rapidly exchanged between the two friends. But certainly they could only make plausible guesses and they were soon lost in the shadows of this mystery.

"Let's have a look at the note-book . . ." John Cort suggested.

"Yes, that's all we can do," Max Huber agreed. "Perhaps, lacking definite information, even if there are only dates, we may be able to work out . . ."

John Cort opened the note-book, whose pages were stuck together by the damp. "I don't think that this is going to tell us very much," he commented.

"Why?"

"Because all the pages are blank . . . except for the first, that is . . ."

"And that first page, John? . . ."

A few short phrases . . . and a few dates which no doubt would enable the doctor to compile his journal later."

And with some difficulty John Cort succeeded in deciphering the following lines. They were written in pencil in German and he translated them as he went along:

"29th July, 1896—Arrived with escort at a clearing in the Oubanghi Forest . . . Encamped on the right bank of the river . . . Built our raft.

"3rd August—Raft completed . . . sent the escort back

to Nghila . . . Destroyed all traces of the camp . . . Embarked with my servant.

"9th August—Went down the river for seven days . . . Stopped at a clearing . . . Many monkeys in the neighbourhood . . . Place seemed suitable.

"10th August—Landed the stores . . . Selected a place to erect the hut-cage beneath the trees on the river bank, at the end of a clearing . . . Monkeys numerous, chimpanzees, gorillas.

"13th August—Encampment completed . . . Took possession of the hut . . . Neighbourhood completely deserted . . . No trace of human beings, natives or otherwise . . . Water-birds quite abundant . . . Stream full of fishes . . . Well sheltered in the hut during a squall.

"25th August—Twenty-seven days elapsed . . . Life regularly organised . . . A few hippopotami on the surface of the stream, but no aggression on their part . . . Elands and antelopes brought down . . . Large monkeys came last night quite close to the hut . . . What kind are they? That cannot yet be made out . . . They made no hostile demonstrations, sometimes running about on the ground, sometimes swinging among the trees . . . Thought a fire could be seen about a hundred paces away in the undergrowth . . . Strange fact to be verified: It seems that these monkeys are certainly talking, that they are exchanging a few words . . . A little one said *Ngora! . . . Ngora!* . . . a word which the natives use in talking of their mother."

Llanga listened attentively to what his friend John was reading and he suddenly exclaimed: "Yes . . . Yes . . . *Ngora* . . . *Ngora* . . . Mother . . . Ngora! . . ."

At this word, noted down by Dr. Johausen and repeated by the little boy, how could John Cort fail to remember that it had reached his ears during the previous night? . . . Believing that it was an illusion or some mistake, he had said nothing about this incident

THE VILLAGE IN THE TREETOPS

to his companions. But after what the Doctor had noted he thought it best to mention it.

So when Max Huber said: "Really, was Professor Garner right? ... talking monkeys! ..."

"All I can tell you, my dear Max, is that I too have heard that word '*Ngora*,'" John Cort declared. And he told them the circumstances in which that word had been uttered by a plaintive voice during the night of the 14th while he was on guard.

"Well, well," said Max Huber, "that's really out of the ordinary...."

"Isn't that what you were asking for, my friend?" John Cort enquired.

Khamis had been listening to what they were saying; what interested the two white men seemed to leave him cold. The facts regarding Dr. Johausen he received with indifference: the great thing was that the Doctor had built a raft which they could use, along with the objects they had found in his empty cage. As to knowing what had become of his servant and himself, the foreloper did not realise that there was any need to ask, and still less that anyone could get it into his head to set out across the great forest to find their tracks, at the risk of being carried away, as no doubt they had been. So if Max Huber and John Cort suggested going to look for him, he would do his best to dissuade them, by reminding them that the only thing they had to do was to continue their homeward journey by going downstream as far as the Oubanghi.

Common sense pointed out, too, that such an attempt would have no chance of success ... In what direction were they to go to find the German doctor? ... If any traces were still left of him. John Cort might have thought it his duty to go to his rescue and Max Huber might have regarded himself as an instrument for saving his life under the direction of Providence? ... But nothing, nothing but these curt phrases in the notebook of which the last appeared under the date of 25th

August, nothing but blank pages which were vainly turned over as far as the last!

So John Cort decided: "There's no doubt at all that the doctor arrived here on the ninth August and that these notes ended on the twenty-fifth of the same month. If he's written nothing since that date it must be because, for one reason or another, he had left his hut, where he had stayed only thirteen days..."

"And," Khamis added, "it's hardly possible to guess what's become of him."

"Never mind," Max Huber commented, "I'm not inquisitive...."

"Oh, my friend, you are, and very much so..."

"You're quite right, John, and to find out the answer to this riddle..."

"Let's get away," was all that the foreloper said.

And indeed they ought not to delay. To get the raft prepared and go down stream, that was what they had to do. If, later, on, they thought it proper to organise an expedition for Dr. Johausen's benefit, to venture into the very depths of the great forest, that could be done under more favourable conditions, and the two friends would be free to take part in it.

Before leaving the cage, Khamis investigated its furthest corners. Perhaps he would find something useful within it. There would be nothing improper in this, for after two years' absence, how could they suppose that its owner would ever reappear to reclaim it?...

The hut was strongly built and still afforded an excellent shelter. The zinc roof, covered with a thatch, had resisted the bad weather. The front wall, the only one to be barred, faced eastwards and was sheltered from the strong wind. The furniture would probably have still been intact if it had not been taken away—which certainly seemed quite inexplicable. After the hut had been left empty for two years a few repairs would admittedly have been necessary. The planks of the side walls were getting loose, the feet of the uprights

THE VILLAGE IN THE TREETOPS

were rickety in the damp earth, signs of dilapidation were visible beneath the festoons of lianas and leaves. But this was a task which Khamis and his companions did not have to undertake. That this hut would ever again form a refuge for some other enthusiast for the study of monkeys, that was quite improbable. So it could be left just as it was.

But could they not find some other objects besides those which they had already picked up? Khamis looked for them carefully. No weapons, no tools, no boxes, no preserved food, no clothing. So the foreloper would have come away empty-handed had he not noticed that when he stamped in a further corner of the hut the ground had a metallic ring.

"There's something here," he said.

"Perhaps it's a key?" Max Huber suggested.

"And why a key?" John Cort asked.

"Oh, my dear John . . . the key of the mystery!"

It was not however a key; it was a tinned-iron case which had been buried in that corner and which Khamis dug up. It did not seem to have been damaged, and it was not without great satisfaction that the man realised that it contained a hundred cartridges!

"Thank you, my good doctor," Max Huber exclaimed, "and perhaps one day we'll be able to return the signal service which you've rendered us!"

A signal service indeed, for the cartridges were the same calibre as their carbines.

All that was now needed to do was to go back to their stopping-place, and to get the raft into a navigable condition.

"But first," John Cort suggested, "let's see if there isn't any trace left anywhere of Dr. Johausen and his servant . . . It's possible that they were both carried off into the depths of the forest by the natives, but it's just as possible that they fell while defending themselves . . . And that their remains have never been buried . . ."

JULES VERNE

"Then it will be our duty to bury them," Max pointed out.

A search carried out over a radius of a hundred yards gave no result. They had to conclude that the hapless Johausen had been kidnapped—and by whom, if it were not by the natives, the very ones whom the doctor had taken for monkeys and whom he had heard talking? . . . Were there any signs indeed that such creatures were endowed with speech? . . .

"Anyhow," John Cort commented, "this suggests that the Oubanghi forest is frequented by wandering tribes, and we shall have to keep a look-out."

"Just as you say, Mr. John," Khamis agreed, "now let's go to the raft . . ."

"And still not knowing what's become of the worthy Teuton!" Max Huber replied. "Wherever can he be? . . ."

"Where people are who are never heard of again," John Cort told him.

"And what sort of an answer is that, John?"

"It's the only one that we can give, my dear Max."

When they first went back to the cave it was about nine o'clock and Khamis first got busy preparing lunch. As they now had a saucepan, Max Huber suggested that they should substitute boiled for roast or grilled meat; that would vary their everyday menu. The suggestion was accepted, the fire was lighted, and, about noon, the guests enjoyed a soup which lacked nothing except bread, vegetables and salt.

Before lunch they had got busy repairing the raft and they continued their work after it. Khamis had found behind the hut a few planks to replace those of the platform, which had rotted in several places; thus a difficult task had been avoided, considering their lack of tools. The collection of beams and planks was bound together by means of lianas as solid as iron bands or at least as ropes. The work was complete by the time the sun disappeared behind the clumps on the right bank of the stream.

THE VILLAGE IN THE TREETOPS

Their departure had been postponed until next day at dawn. It would be better to spend the night in the cave, and indeed the rain which had been threatening began to fall violently about eight o'clock.

Thus, after having found a place where Dr. Johausen had meant to settle down, the three men had to go without knowing what had become of him! . . . Nothing . . . Nothing . . . Not even a trace! . . . This thought never ceased to obsess Max Huber, although John Cort cared little about it and it left the foreloper completely indifferent.

Huber went off into dreams of baboons, chimpanzees, gorillas, mandrils, and talking monkeys, assuming that is, that the doctor had not been dealing with the natives! . . . And then—imaginative as he was!—the great forest appeared before him with all its strange possibilities, its improbable haunts which brought to mind its mysterious depths, its unheard-of-peoples, its unknown types, the whole villages lost beneath its great trees . . .

Before stretching himself out in the depths of the cave: "My dear John," he said, "and you too, Khamis, I've got something to suggest."

"And what's that, Max?"

"It's to do something for the doctor . . ."

"Not to go and look for him?" the foreloper protested.

"No," Max Huber explained, "but to give his name to this stream. I presume it hasn't got one."

And that is how the Rio Johausen was in future to appear on the modern maps of Equatorial Africa.

The night was calm, and, while they kept watch in turn, neither John Cort nor Max Huber nor Khamis heard so much as one word reach their ear.

CHAPTER IX

DOWN THE RIO JOHAUSEN

It was half past six in the morning when, on 16th March, the raft cast off its moorings, left the bank, and went down the Rio Johausen.

It was hardly daylight but already dawn was breaking. Clouds were rushing across the higher regions of the air under the influence of a strong wind. Rain was no longer threatening but the weather remained murky throughout the day. This gave Khamis and his companions nothing to complain of, for they were going to descend a stream which otherwise would have been open to the perpendicular rays of the sun.

The raft, oblong in shape, measured only seven or eight feet wide and about a dozen feet in length, just big enough for four passengers and the objects they were taking with them. There was little in their cargo: the metal box of cartridges, the weapons, including three carbines, the saucepan, the mug, the cup. The three revolvers were of smaller calibre than the rifles, and could be used only for about twenty shots, taking into account the cartridges which John Cort and Max Huber carried in their pockets. On the whole there was reason to hope that the ammunition would not run out before the hunters reached the banks of the Oubanghi.

In the prow of the raft, on a layer of earth carefully piled up, was placed a heap of dry wood which could easily be renewed should Khamis need a fire outside of the hours when they halted. In the stern a strong steering-oar, made of one of the planks, allowed the

THE VILLAGE IN THE TREETOPS

raft to be guided or at all events to be kept in the main current of the stream.

Between the two banks, which were about fifty yards apart, the current was moving with a speed of roughly half a mile an hour. With this speed the raft would take twenty to thirty days to cover the 250 miles which separated the travellers from the Oubanghi. If this was not nearly as fast as they could have made their way through the forest, at least the journey would not tire them.

As to any obstacles which might bar the course of the Rio, they did not know what to expect. What they realised at the outset, however, was that the river-bed was deep and sinuous, so that they had to watch their course very carefully. If waterfalls or rapids were to obstruct their way, the foreloper would act according to circumstances.

Until the mid-day halt the navigation was easily carried out, and the eddies and the points of the rocks were easy to avoid. Thanks to the skill of Khamis, who corrected its direction with a thrust of his vigorous arm, the raft did not run aground even once.

John Cort posted in the bow with his carbine beside him, was watching the shores with a hunter's keen interest. He was thinking of renewing the stock of food: if any feathered or furred game were to come within range, it would be easy to bring it down.

This indeed happened at about half past nine. A bullet brought down a water-buck, a kind of antelope which frequents the eddies of the rivers.

"Good shot!" exclaimed Max Huber.

"A useless shot," John Cort declared, "if we can't get hold of the animal..."

"That will only take a few moments," the foreloper replied.

And, leaning on his steering-oar, he took the raft into the bank near a tiny patch of sand on which the water-

JULES VERNE

buck was lying. The animal was cut up and the pieces kept to serve for the next few meals.

From time to time, Max Huber turned to account his skill as a fisherman, although he had at his service only very crude appliances, two lengths of string which they had found in the Doctor's cage, and, as hooks, some spines of acacia baited with fragments of flesh. Would the fish, which they could see appearing at the surface of the water, decide to bite? . . . Max Huber was kneeling on the starboard side of the raft and Llanga, standing at his side, was watching the operation with keen interest.

The pike of the Rio Johausen must be as greedy as they are stupid, for one of them showed no delay in swallowing the hook. After playing it much as the natives do the hippopotamus which they capture in a similar manner, Max Huber was skilful enough to bring it in. This fish weighed a good eight or nine pounds, and certainly the travellers were not going to wait until the next day to feast upon it.

At the mid-day halt, lunch consisted of roast waterbuck-steak and the pike, of which nothing was left but the bones. For dinner it was agreed that they would make a stew with the antelope's leg. And, as this would need several hours' cooking, the foreloper kindled his fire in the prow of the raft and stood the saucepan on the flames. Then the voyage went on without interruption until evening.

During the afternoon fishing yielded no further results, and about six Khamis came to a standstill beside a little rocky shore shaded by the lower branches of a gum tree. It was an excellent place in which to make a halt, for mussels and other shellfish abounded between the rocks. Some cooked and others eaten raw, they made an agreeable conclusion to the evening meal. With three or four fragments of biscuit and a pinch of salt, the feast would have left nothing to desire.

As the night threatened to be dark, the foreloper

THE VILLAGE IN THE TREETOPS

was unwilling to abandon himself to the current. The Rio Johausen occasionally swept along enormous tree-trunks, and the mere touch of these could have done much damage to the raft. So the travellers made their beds at the foot of a gum-tree on a layer of grass; and, thanks to the watch they kept up in turn by the three men, the camp did not receive any troublesome visitors. The only thing was that the howling of the monkeys never stopped from sunset to sunrise.

"And I dare maintain that those fellows aren't talking!" commented Max Huber. At daybreak he went to plunge into the clear waters of the river his face and his hands, which the malevolent mosquitoes had not spared.

That morning a heavy rain was falling and the start was put off for a good hour. It would obviously be better to avoid these downpours which fall from the sky so frequently in the equatorial region of Africa, and the thick foliage of the gum-tree to a certain extent protected not only the camp but the raft, which had been moored to the front of its strong roots. What was more, the weather was stormy, and on the surface of the river the drops of water were producing a flash like tiny electric bulbs; and although there was no lightning a few growls of thunder were rolling overhead. Hail was not to be feared, for the immense African forests are thick enough to check its fall.

The state of the weather was so alarming that John Cort thought he had better come to a decision: "If this rain doesn't stop," he pointed out, "we'd better stay where we are . . . we've got plenty of ammunition . . . our cartridge belts are full but it will be a change of clothing we shall lack . . ."

"So," laughed Max Huber, "why not dress after the style of the country . . . in human skin? . . . That would simplify things! . . . To wash our linen all we should have to do would be to bathe, and to brush our clothing we need only rub against the branches!"

And indeed for the last week the two friends, not being able to get a change of underwear, had done their own laundrywork.

Yet the downpour was so violent that it lasted only an hour, during which they took the opportunity of making their breakfast. In this meal there appeared a new dish and one which they welcomed; some newly-laid bustards' eggs which Llanga had found and which Khamis boiled in the saucepan. And once again Max Huber complained, not unreasonably, that Mother Nature had been very negligent in not putting into the eggs the grain of salt without which they could not be enjoyed.

At about half past seven the rain stopped, although the sky was still stormy. So the raft regained the current in the midst of the stream.

Fishing-lines were trailed behind it, and several fish were obliging enough to bite in time to form part of the mid-day meal.

Khamis suggested that, so as to retrieve the morning's delay, they should do without the regular mid-day halt. His idea being accepted, John Cort lit the fire and soon the saucepan was singing on the glowing embers. As there was still a good supply of the water-buck, their guns kept silent, though more than once Max Huber was tempted by the game which was roaming along the river banks.

This part of the forest was indeed very rich in game, not only in waterfowl, but in animals, including giraffes, whose flesh is quite eatable. It would have been easy to bring some of them down, but what would be the good, as the hunters had plenty of food for the following day? And certainly it would have been useless to overload and encumber the raft, as John Cort pointed out to his friend.

"What do you expect, my dear John?" Max Huber declared. "My rifle comes up to my shoulder of itself when I can see such splendid shots within range."

THE VILLAGE IN THE TREETOPS

But as this would be only to shoot for the sake of shooting—although this consideration might not have been enough to check a real hunter—Max Huber hinted to his carbine that it had better keep quiet and not to rise to his shoulder of itself. So the woods did not echo to sudden explosions, and the raft made its way quietly down the Rio Johausen.

But the three hunters were able to make up for this during the afternoon. Their firearms had to make their voices heard—but speaking in defence and not in attack.

During the morning about eight miles had been covered, and the river was then making a number of sudden swerves, although its general direction was still towards the south-west. It irregular banks were covered with enormous trees whose branches almost reached the surface of the water.

Although the river was no narrower, although it was still fifty to sixty yards wide, the lower branches of the trees met overhead and formed a cradle of greenery beneath which the ripples murmured. Several of these branches, intertwined at their ends, were attached by means of serpentine lianas; this formed a bridge of vegetation across which agile clowns, or at least monkeys, could have made their way from bank to bank.

The storm clouds had not yet left the horizon, but the sun was high in the sky and its rays were falling vertically downwards on to the river, so that Khamis and his comrades were bound to appreciate the value of this journey beneath a thick dome of verdure. It suggested a walk through the undergrowth of the shady forest without any fatigue and without the embarrassment of a soil bristling with spiky grass.

"Certainly it's a regular park, this Oubanghi forest," John Cort declared, "a park with its clumps of trees and its flowing waters! Anyone would think we were in one of the National Parks of the United States amid the sources of the Missouri or in the Yellowstone!"

"A park where monkeys swarm!" commented Max

JULES VERNE

Huber, "anybody would think that the whole of the simian race were meeting here! We're in the kingdom of the apes, where chimpanzees, gorillas, and gibbons reign in all sovereignty!"

This observation was justified by the enormous numbers of these animals which were occupying the shores, appearing on the trees, and running and gambolling about in the depths of the forest. Never had any of the travellers encountered so many of them nor seen them so turbulent or making so many contortions. What cries, what leaps, what somersaults, and what a series of grimaces, a photographer would have been able to capture with his lens!

"After all," Max Huber added, "nothing could be more natural! Aren't we in the center of Africa? Well, between the natives and the apes of the Congo—except for Khamis, that's understood—I don't think there's very much difference."

"But you have to remember," John Cort replied, "that the distinction between the man and the animals is that one is equipped with intelligence and that the other is dominated by an impersonal instinct..."

"The latter is much more certain than the former, my dear John!"

"I don't say no, Max. But these two factors of life are separated by a gulf, and as this has never been crossed the evolutionists have no grounds to claim that man is descended from the monkeys..."

"Quite right," Max Huber agreed, "and there is still lacking a rung in that ladder, a creature midway between the anthropoids and man, with a little less instinct and a little more intelligence. And even if it did exist the question raised by this Darwinian Theory would still remain to be settled, in my opinion at any rate."

But at that time they had something better to do than to try to solve, by quoting the axiom that nature never makes leaps, the question of knowing whether all the

THE VILLAGE IN THE TREETOPS

living creatures are akin. What they had to do was to take precautions or more active measures against any hostile manifestations from a race fearsome by its numerical superiority.

It would have been very imprudent indeed to neglect this. These apes formed an army which seemed to have been recruited from all the monkey population of the Oubanghi. Their demonstrations could not be misunderstood and the travellers might have to defend themselves to the bitter end.

The foreloper could not observe this noisy stir without being seriously disquieted. This was shown by the rush of blood to his face, by the way he lowered his thick eyebrows, from his keen glances from side to side, from his forehead, which was crossed by deep wrinkles.

"Let's keep ready," he said, "our carbines loaded and our cartridges within reach . . . I can't see how things are going to turn out."

"Bah! a shot or two will soon make them disappear," replied Max Huber, as he raised his carbine to his shoulder.

"Don't shoot, Mr. Max!" exclaimed Khamis, "we mustn't attack them . . . we mustn't provoke them! . . . It will be quite enough to have to defend ourselves!"

"But they're beginning . . ." replied John Cort.

"Don't reply unless we have to!" Khamis urged them again.

The attack was not long in livening up. From the river bank came stones and pieces of wood, hurled by large apes endowed with colossal strength. They also threw more inoffensive projectiles, including fruits torn from the trees.

The foreloper tried to keep the raft in the middle of the current and almost at the same distance from each of the banks, so as to make the projectiles less dangerous and less sure in aim. Unfortunately there was no means of sheltering against this attack. What was more, the number of the assailants was increasing, and several of the missiles had already hit the travellers, though fortunately without doing them any harm.

"That's quite enough of that," Max Huber said at last; taking aim at a gorilla who had appeared among the reeds he brought it down with a shot.

The sound of the explosion was replied to by a deafening clamour but the attack did not cease nor did the hordes take to flight. And certainly to exterminate these monkeys one by one the ammunition would not nearly have sufficed: with only one bullet to every ape their stock would soon have been exhausted. And then what could the hunters do with their cartridge-belts empty?

"Don't fire any more," John Cort gave the order, "all that it does is to excite these cursed animals! We'll get away, let us hope with a few unimportant bruises..."

"Many thanks!" replied Max Huber, who had just been hit in the leg by a stone.

They went on down the river followed by this double escort on the banks, which were very sinuous in this part of the Rio Johausen. In certain narrowings, moreover, they were so close together that the breadth of the river-bed was reduced by a third. The progress of the raft quickened with the increased speed of the current.

But perhaps when night fell the attack might come to an end? Perhaps the assailants might scatter across the forest? Nevertheless, if he had to, instead of stopping for the evening halt Khamis would risk travelling until day-break. But it was still barely four o'clock and until seven the situation would continue to be very disquieting.

And, indeed, what made it worse was that the raft was not safe from being invaded. Though monkeys like water no more than cats, though there was nothing to fear from their trying to swim, the arrangement of the branches above the river would in some places enable them to venture out on these leafy bridges and lianas, and then to let themselves drop on the head of Khamis

THE VILLAGE IN THE TREETOPS

and his companions. That would be only child's play for animals as agile as they were ill-disposed.

This manoeuvre was indeed attempted, about five o'clock by five or six large gorillas, at a bend in the river where the trees met overhead. Posted about fifty yards down-stream, these animals were waiting for the raft to pass by. John Cort noticed them and nobody could mistake their intentions.

"They're going to fall on top of us," exclaimed Max Huber, "and if we don't make them clear out . . ."

"Fire!" the foreloper gave the order.

Three explosions rang out, and three apes, mortally wounded, after having tried to hang on to the branches, dropped into the river.

In the midst of a more violent clamour, a score or so of monkeys climbed up on the lianas ready to hurl themselves on to the raft.

The weapons had to be reloaded and fired without losing an instant. A withering fusillade followed. A dozen or so gorillas and chimpanzees were wounded before the raft passed under this bridge of vegetation, and the others fled discouraged to the banks.

The travellers might have reflected that if Professor Garner had settled down in the depths of the mighty forest, his fate would have been that of Dr. Johausen. Assuming that the latter had been welcomed by this forest population in the same style as themselves, did it need any more to explain his disappearance? Nonetheless, if he had been attacked certain signs of this would have been visible: thanks to the destructive instincts of the monkeys, the cage would have not remained intact and there would have been nothing but scattered fragments in the place where it had stood.

But after all at this moment the most urgent thing to worry about was not the fate of the German doctor but what would happen to the raft. For indeed the width of the rio was gradually diminishing. A hundred yards away on the right, just in front of a rocky point, the swirling water indicated a powerful eddy. If the raft were to fall into it and no longer be subject to the action of the current which the point was turning aside, it would be carried into the bank.

Khamis did the best he could to keep the raft in the current with his steering-oar; to get it out of the eddy would be very difficult and the monkeys on the right bank would come in large numbers to attack it. So they would have to be put to flight with bullets, and the carbines came into action the moment the raft begun to spin around.

But an instant later the horde had disappeared, though it had been neither bullets nor explosions which had dispersed them. For about an hour a storm had been rising towards the zenith and livid clouds now covered the sky. Suddenly flashes of lightning lit up the air and the thunderstorm unchained itself with that prodigious speed peculiar to the low latitudes.

At these terrible outbursts the apes felt that instinctive trouble which electricity inspires in every animal. Overcome with fear, they went to seek under the thickest clumps of trees a shelter against these dazzling flashes, this formidable tearing asunder of the clouds. In a few minutes the two banks had been deserted, and of the whole horde there remained only a score of lifeless bodies stretched out amongst the reeds on the banks.

CHAPTER X

NGORA!

NEXT MORNING the sky had cleared—or rather it had been dusted by the powerful brush of the storm—and its vault of clear blue appeared above the treetops. At sunrise the tiny drops of water on the leaves and grass evaporated and the ground soon dried up enough to lend itself to travel. But there was no question of continuing their journey towards the south-west on foot and if the Rio Johausen did not swerve from that direction, Khamis felt no doubt that in about three weeks he would reach the Oubanghi Basin.

The violent atmospheric disturbance, its thousands of lightning flashes, its prolonged rolls of thunder, its torrents of rain, had not stopped until three in the morning. After having reached the bank on the other side of the eddy the raft had found shelter. In that place rose a gigantic baobab whose trunk was so much decayed that it was held together only by its bark. By crowding together, Khamis and his comrades managed to get inside it, taking with them their modest equipment of utensils, weapons and munitions, which must not be allowed to suffer from the storm and which could easily be re-embarked when it was time to set off.

"My word, it came just at the right time, that storm did!" commented John Cort. He was conversing with Max while the foreloper was getting the remains of the meat ready for the first meal. While talking the two young men busied themselves with cleaning their carbines, an indispensable task after the lively fusillade of the previous day.

Meanwhile Llanga was ferreting about in the midst of the reeds and the grass, looking for nests and eggs.

"Yes, my dear John, the storm did come just at the right time," said Max Huber, "and Heaven send that those abominable brutes do not take it into their heads to reappear now that it's over! Anyhow, let's keep our guard."

Khamis was somewhat apprehensive that at daybreak the apes would return to the two banks. But soon he was reassured when as the dawn penetrated the undergrowth they could hear no suspicious sound.

"I've gone down the bank about a hundred yards and

JULES VERNE

I haven't seen any of the monkeys," John Cort assured his friends.

"That's a good sign," replied Max Huber, "and in future I hope we can use our cartridges otherwise than in defending ourselves against them! I was afraid we were going to have to use up all our reserve."

"And how could we renew them?" asked John Cort, "we can't count upon another cage to furnish us with bullets and powder and shot."

"Well," exclaimed Max Huber, "when I think that our good doctor wanted to get into social relations with such beings! . . . A fine lot they are! . . . As for finding out what words they would use for inviting each other to dinner and how they wish each other good morning or good evening, you really need a Professor Garner of the sort there are in America, or a Doctor Johausen of the sort there are in Germany, and maybe even in France."

"In France, Max?"

"Oh, if you were to search among the savants of the Institute or the Sorbonne, you'd soon find some Idio . . ."

"Idiot!" John Cort protested.

"Idiom-ographer," Max Huber completed the word, "who would be capable of coming into the Congo forests to take up the work of Professor Garner and Doctor Johausen!"

"Anyhow, my dear Max, if we feel reassured as regards the former, who seems to have broken off relations with monkey society, that's not at all the case with the latter and I'm very much afraid . . ."

"That the baboons or something have broken his bones!" Max Huber finished the sentence for him. "Judging by the way they welcomed us yesterday, we can easily tell whether they're civilised or ever likely to become so!"

"Look here, Max, I take it that the animals are going to stay animals . . ."

"And men too!" Max Huber smiled. "All the same I

THE VILLAGE IN THE TREETOPS

feel very sorry at having to return to Libreville without bringing back some tidings of the doctor."

"I quite agree, but the important thing is for us to be able to get through this interminable forest."

"We'll do that all right."

"Yes, but I wish we had done it already!"

Anyhow the journey seemed to give a fairly good chance of being completed, for all the raft had to do was to abandon itself to the current. It would however be necessary for the bed of the Rio Johausen not to be encumbered with rapids, cut by reefs, or interrupted by water-falls. That was what the foreloper especially dreaded.

He now called his companions to breakfast, and Llanga appeared almost immediately, bringing a few ducks' eggs, which were kept for the mid-day meal. Thanks to the remains of the antelope there would be no need to renew the store of game before the halt at noon.

"Well, I should think," John Cort suggested, "so as not to waste our ammunition, why not feast on the flesh of the monkeys?"

"Ugh!" was all that Max Huber said.

"Look how disgusted he is!"

"What, my dear John, gorilla cutlets, gibbon fillets, chimpanzee legs, or a fricassee of mandrils..."

"That wouldn't be bad," Khamis declared, "the natives don't turn up their nose at a meal of this sort."

"And I should eat it if I had to," said John Cort.

"Cannibal!" Max Huber exclaimed, "to eat your fellows..."

"Many thanks, Max!"

They ended up by leaving to the birds of prey the apes which they had killed in the battle. The Oubanghi forest contained enough game and poultry for there to be no need to pay the representatives of the monkey tribe the honour of introducing them into a human stomach.

JULES VERNE

Khamis found serious difficulties in getting the raft out of the eddy and in doubling the point.

They all lent a hand in this manoeuvre, which took almost an hour. They had to cut down some small trees and to strip them of their branches to make punting-poles by which to get clear of the bank. The raft was still in the eddy, and if the hordes were to return at this moment it would not be possible to evade their attack by pushing out into the current. Certainly neither the foreloper nor his companions would have come unscathed out of so an unequal a struggle.

But after a thousand efforts the raft skirted the end of the point and went on its way down the Rio Johausen.

The day promised to be fine; no signs of a storm on the horizon, no threat of rain. On the other hand a shower of solar rays fell vertically upon them, and the heat would have been torrid but for a lively breeze from the north which would have given the raft much help if only this had had a sail.

The further it went to the south-west the broader the river became. No leafy cradle now stretched over its bed, no more branches intermingled from bank to bank. In these circumstances it was not so likely that the apes on its banks would be so dangerous as they had the previous day. Anyhow, they did not show themselves.

Yet the banks of the stream were not deserted. There were many aquatic birds enlivening them with their cries, and John Cort brought down several brace of them. These would serve for the mid-day meal, along with the eggs which the boy discovered. So as to make up for lost time they did not stop at the usual hour, and the first half of the day ended without the slightest incident. In the afternoon, not without good reason, there was an alarm.

It was four o'clock when Khamis, who was holding the steering-oar at the stern, asked John Cort to take his place and went into the bow of the raft. Max Huber

THE VILLAGE IN THE TREETOPS

got up, made certain that nothing seemed to be threatening them on either of the banks and asked tthe foreloper, "What are you looking at?"

"That," and Khamis pointed downstream towards a fairly violent movement of the waters.

"Another eddy," said Max Huber, "or rather a sort of river maëlstrom! Look out, Khamis, and see we don't get drawn into it."

"It isn't an eddy," the foreloper declared.

"What is it, then?"

This question was replied to at once by a sort of liquid jet which spurted about ten feet above the surface of the stream.

Completely surprised, Max Huber asked: "Are there by any chance whales in the rivers of Central Africa?"

"No . . . Hippopotami!" the foreloper replied.

A noisy snort was heard, and at the same moment there emerged from the water an enormous head with its jaws armed with powerful teeth.

The hippopotamus is a fearsome animal though not specially ferocious, but when for one reason or another it gets excited or when it is in pain, when for example it has been harpooned, it loses its temper, it hurls itself furiously against its hunters, it chases them along the banks, it throws itself on their canoe, which it is powerful enough to sink or to rip open with its jaws strong enough to amputate an arm or a leg.

None of the travellers on the raft—not even Max Huber, enthusiastic hunter though he was—had any idea of attacking such a creature. To be sure, the creature might want to attack them and if it reached the raft, if it hurled itself upon it, if it bore down on it with its weight of perhaps four thousand pounds or ripped it apart with its terrible fangs, what would become of Khamis and his companions?

At this point the current was rapid, and it might be better to content themselves with following it instead of making for one of the banks; the hippopotamus might

JULES VERNE

have gone after them. On land, it is true, its attack would have been easier to avoid, for it is unsuited for rapid movement with its short thick legs and its enormous stomach which brushes against the ground. It is more like a pig than a wild boar. But on the surface of the river the raft would be at its mercy. It would rip it into fragments, and even if the travellers could manage to swim to the banks, what a disaster it would be if they had to build a second floating contrivance!

"We'll try to get by without being seen," was Khamis' advice. "Let's stretch ourselves out, don't let's make any noise and let's be ready to fling ourselves into the water if we have to..."

"I'll look after you, Llanga," Max Huber assured the boy.

They followed the foreloper's advice, each of them lying down on the raft, which the current was sweeping along with some speed. In that position perhaps they had a chance of not being seen by the hippopotamus.

Then came a loud snort, a sort of porcine grunt, which they heard a few minutes later, just as the swaying bulk of the raft showed that they were crossing the water disturbed by the gigantic animal.

There were several seconds of acute anxiety. Would the raft be raised out of the water by the monster's head, or submerged by its great bulk?

The travellers did not feel reassured until the disturbance of the water ceased, and at the same time there lessened the noise of the snorting, who's warm breath they had felt as they went by. When they got up they could no longer see the monster, which had plunged back into the depths of the river.

To be sure, hunters who were accustomed to struggle with the elephant, and who had just been on an expedition with Urdax' caravan, would never have been frightened to meet a hippopotamus. They had several times attacked these animals in the marshes of the Upper Oubanghi, but under more favourable conditions.

THE VILLAGE IN THE TREETOPS

On board this frail collection of planks whose loss would have been so regrettable, their fears may well be understood, and they were lucky to have escaped attack by that formidable brute.

In the evening Khamis stopped at the mouth of a stream which emerged on the left bank. They could not have chosen a better place to spend the night, at the foot of a clump of banana trees whose great leaves would give them shelter.

There too, the shore was covered with edible molluscs; these were collected and eaten raw or cooked, according to their species. As for the bananas, their juice, mingled with the water of the stream, would form a refreshing drink.

"This would be quite perfect," commented Max Huber, "if we were certain of sleeping in peace . . . Unfortunately there are these cursèd insects and they'll take good care not to spare us . . . For lack of a mosquito-net we shall wake up covered with stings!"

And indeed this is certainly what would have happened if Llanga had not found a method of driving away the myriads of mosquitoes which had gathered in buzzing clouds.

He had gone up the river bank, and his voice could be heard a short distance away.

Khamis went up to him, and Llanga pointed to some heaps of dried manure left by the animals who had come to drink at that spot.

To throw this material on to the flames, thus producing a thick acrid smoke, would be the best method, and maybe the only method, of driving away the mosquitoes, and the natives use it whenever they can.

A few minutes later a big pile had been heaped up at the foot of the banana tree. The fire had been rekindled with dead wood and the foreloper threw some of the dung on to it. A cloud of thick smoke arose and the air was at once cleared of these intolerable insects.

The fire had to be kept up all night by the three men,

JULES VERNE

who took it in turns to watch. So next morning, restored by good sleep, they set off at daybreak down the Rio Johausen.

Nothing is more variable than the weather in the climate of Central Africa. To the clear sky of the previous evening there followed greyish clouds, which threatened a rainy day. Admittedly as the clouds were low only a fine rain would fall, a mere liquid dust, but this would be very disagreeable to receive.

Fortunately, Khamis had had a good idea. The leaves of the banana trees are perhaps the largest in the whole vegetable kingdom, and the blacks use them for the roofs of their huts.

Using only a dozen and binding together the stems by means of the lianas, the travellers could build a sort of shelter in the middle of the raft. That was what the foreloper did before they set out. So the passengers were sheltered from that rain, which flowed off the surface of the leaves.

During the first half of the day a few monkeys appeared on the right bank; about a score of them were of large size and they seemed inclined to recommence their hostilities of two days before. The wisest thing was to avoid any contact with them, and the travellers succeeded in keeping the raft near the left bank, which was less frequented by the hordes of apes.

John Cort quite rightly pointed out that relations must be rare between the monkey tribes of the two banks, as communication could only be carried out by the bridges of twigs and lianas, hardly practicable even by monkeys.

The raft did not halt for the mid-day meal, and during the afternoon it stopped only once. This was to embark an antelope which John Cort had brought down behind a clump of reeds near a bend in the river.

Here, swerving off towards the south-east, the Rio Johausen flowed almost at right-angles to its usual course. This gave Khamis some anxiety, for he could see

THE VILLAGE IN THE TREETOPS

himself being carried away into the heart of the forest, whereas his goat was in the opposite direction, towards the Atlantic.

Certainly they could not doubt that the Rio Johausen was one of the tributaries of the Oubanghi; but to seek for that confluence several hundred miles inland in the very heart of the Independent Congo, how far it would take them out of their way! Fortunately, after an hour's travel the foreloper, thanks to his sense of direction—for the sun was not visible—realised that the stream had regained its former course. They might well hope that it would bring the raft across the boundary of the French Congo, from which it would be easy to reach Libreville.

At half past six, by a vigorous thrust of the steering-oar, Khamis reached the left bank in the depths of a narrow creek, sheltered by the great foliage of a tree something like a mahogany.

Though the rain was no longer falling, the sky was not yet clear of those fogs which the sun had not been able to pierce. It need not be assumed that the night was cold; a thermometer would have marked 26°C. The fire was soon crackling among the stones of the creek, but that was only for the demands of cooking, to roast a haunch of antelope.

This time Llanga had vainly sought for molluscs to vary the menu or for bananas to flavour the waters of the Rio Johausen. On the other hand, the travellers knew how to get rid of the mosquitoes, by the same method as before.

At half past seven, it was not yet night and a vague gleam was reflected on the waters of the river, while on their surface floated a tangle of leaves and plants and tree-trunks, torn away from the banks.

While the three men were preparing their beds by piling up armfuls of dry grass at the foot of the tree, Llanga was coming and going on the bank, amusing himself by following that drift of floating wreckage.

JULES VERNE

Suddenly there appeared, about thirty fathoms upstream, the trunk of a tree of medium size complete with all its foliage. It had been broken off five or six feet below its fork, and the break was freshly made.

Around its branches, of which the lower ones were dragging in the water, was entangled a thick foliage, including some flowers and fruits which had survived the fall of the tree.

This tree had most probably been struck by lightning during the recent storm. From the place where its roots were embedded it had fallen on to the bank; then, gradually sliding towards the water, having worked itself clear of the reeds and been seized by the current, it was drifting with the rest of the débris on the surface of the rio.

It must not be imagined that Llanga would have been able to think this out. He would not even have noticed this tree among the rest of the wreckage which was coming down along with it had his attention not been specially attracted to it.

Indeed, among the branches he thought he could see a living creature, which was making gestures as though appealing for help. But in the semi-darkness he could not distinguish it clearly. Was it some sort of animal? . . .

Feeling quite bewildered, he was going to call Max Huber and John Cort when something else happened.

The trunk was only about forty yards away and was making obliquely towards the creek where the raft had been moored.

Suddenly a cry rang out—a strange cry, or rather a sort of despairing appeal as if some human being were calling for help. Then, as the trunk was passing the creek, that creature hurled itself into the stream with the plain intention of reaching the shore.

Llanga thought he could recognise a child smaller than himself; it must have been on the tree at the very moment when it fell. Did it know how to swim? . . . Very badly anyhow, and not enough to reach the bank.

THE VILLAGE IN THE TREETOPS

Plainly its strength was giving out. It struggled, disappeared, reappeared, and every now and again a sort of gurgle came from its lips.

Obeying the sentiment of humanity and without taking the time to think, Llanga threw himself into the stream and reached the place where the child had gone down for the last time.

At once John Cort and Max Huber, who had heard its first cry, had rushed to the edge of the creek.

Seeing Llanga supporting a body on the surface of the river, they lent a hand to help him get back on the bank.

"Well, Llanga," Max Huber exclaimed, "what have you fished up now?"

"A child . . . my friend Max . . . a child . . . it was drowning . . ."

"A child? . . ." John Cort repeated.

"Yes . . . my friend John," and Llanga knelt down beside the little creature whose life he had certainly saved.

Max Huber bent over it so as to see it more clearly. "Well, it isn't a child!" he declared as he got up.

"What is it then?" asked John Cort.

"A little monkey . . . the offspring of those abominable beasts who attacked us! . . . And it was simply to save it from drowning that you risked drowning yourself, Llanga?"

"A child . . . no . . . a child!" Llanga repeated.

"No, I tell you, and I'll send it back to its family in the depths of the woods."

But whatever his friend Max might say, Llanga insisted that he could see a child in this little creature which owed him life and which had not yet regained consciousness. So, not wanting to be separated from it, he lifted it in his arms, and the others thought that on the whole the best thing was to let him do as he wished.

After having brought the child into the camp, Llanga made certain that it was still breathing; he rubbed it,

JULES VERNE

he warmed it, then he put it down on the dry grass, waiting for its eyes to open.

The night was organised as usual; the two friends were not slow in falling asleep, while Khamis stayed on guard until midnight. But Llanga was unwilling to go to sleep; he was watching over the slightest movement of his protégé.

Stretched beside it, he held its hand, he listened to its breathing . . . and what was his surprise when, about eleven, he heard this word pronounced in a weak voice: "*Ngora . . . Ngora!*" as if that child were calling for its mother!

CHAPTER XI

ON THE NINETEENTH OF MARCH

AT THAT stop they could estimate at a hundred miles the distance which they had covered partly on foot, partly on the raft. Would they have to cover the same distance to reach the Oubanghi? No, in the foreloper's opinion, that second part of the journey would be carried out rapidly so long as no obstacle stopped their navigation.

They embarked at daybreak with their little extra passenger, from whom Llanga did not wish to be separated. After carrying it under the leafy roof, he wanted to stay beside it, hoping that its eyes would open.

That this creature was a member of the ape family of the African Continent, chimpanzee, orang-utang, gorilla, mandril, baboon, or something of the sort—no doubt of this entered the minds of Max Huber or John Cort. They had not even taken the trouble to look at it

THE VILLAGE IN THE TREETOPS

closely, to give it any special attention. It did not much interest them; Llanga had saved it, he wanted to keep it, as anyone might keep a poor dog whom he had picked up out of sheer pity. Very well! For him to have a companion, nothing could be better, and that testified to his good heart. After all, as the two friends had adopted the young native, it was quite in order for him to adopt a little monkey. No doubt as soon as it got a chance of slipping away into the woods, the creature would abandon its rescuer with that ingratitude of which men have by no means the monopoly.

Certainly, if Llanga had come to John Cort or Max Huber, or even to Khamis, and said, "That monkey's talking! it's several times repeated the word '*Ngora*,'" their attention might well have been aroused, to say nothing of their curiosity! . . . Then perhaps they would have examined it more attentively, that little animal! . . . Might they not have discovered that it was a specimen of some race hitherto unknown, that of the talking apes? . . . But Llanga kept silent, afraid that he had been mistaken, that he had heard badly. He promised himself to watch closely over his protégé, and if the word "*Ngora*" or any other word should escape from its lips, then he would tell his friends John and Max.

This was one of the reasons why he stayed under the shelter, trying to give a little food to this tiny creature, which seemed enfeebled by a long fast. No doubt this would not be easy, for the monkeys are fruit-eaters. But Llanga had no fruit whatever to offer it, only antelope flesh, and this would not suit it. What was more, a fairly serious fever kept it from eating and it stayed in a sort of coma.

"And how's your monkey going on?" Max Huber asked Llanga, when the boy showed himself an hour after they started.

"It's still asleep, my friend Max."

"And you mean to keep it?"

"Yes . . . if you'll let me. . . ."

"I don't see anything against it, Llanga. But take care it doesn't scratch you."

"Oh, my friend Max!"

"You've got to look out for it! They're as spiteful as cats, these animals are!"

"Not this one! . . . He's so young! . . . He's got such a sweet little face!"

"Well, as you're going to make a friend of it, you'd better think out a name for it."

"A name? . . . but what?"

"Jacko, of course. All the monkeys are called Jacko!"

This name did not seem to suit Llanga, who said not a word but went back under the shelter.

During that morning navigation was easy and they did not suffer too much from the heat; the layer of cloud was so thick that the sun could not penetrate it. They had reason to be thankful for this, for the Rio Johausen was sometimes flowing through large clearings, and it was impossible to find any shelter along the banks, where the trees were few. The ground became marshy and they would have to skirt it for about a quarter of a mile to right or left to reach the nearest thickets. What they had to fear was that the rain would start falling with its usual violence, but the sky was content with threats.

Though the water-birds were flying in flocks above the marsh, animals hardly showed themselves, to the great annoyance of Max Huber. For the ducks and bustards of the preceding days he would have liked to substitute antelopes, water-bucks, or something of that sort. For this reason, posted in the bow of the raft with his carbine in readiness like a hunter on the look-out, he swept with his glance the shore which the foreloper was approaching, following the whim of the current.

For the mid-day meal they had to content themselves with the legs and wings of birds, and there was nothing surprising that these survivors of the Urdax caravan were getting tired of their daily food. Always meat

THE VILLAGE IN THE TREETOPS

roasted, boiled, or grilled, always fresh water, no fruit, no bread, no salt. Fish, and so badly seasoned! They were longing to arrive on the outskirts of the Oubanghi, where, thanks to the generous hospitality of the missionaries, all these privations would soon be forgotten.

All that day Khamis sought in vain for a suitable place to stop. The banks, bristling with gigantic reeds, seemed quite unapproachable. At their half-soaked base, how would the travellers be able to land? On the other hand, they were making good progress, for the raft never interrupted its journey.

They sailed on thus until five o'clock. Meanwhile John Cort and Max Huber were talking about the incidents of the journey, which had gone on so well for two months. Then had come the return to the clump of tamarisks, the moving flames, the appearance of a formidable horde of elephants, the attack on the caravan, the porters in flight, their leader crushed by the falling tree, the chase by the elephants only halted at the edge of the great forest . . .

"A sad conclusion to a journey hitherto so fortunate!" John Cort ended. "And who knows if it won't be followed by another just as disastrous?"

"That's quite possible, but to my mind it isn't very likely, my dear John."

"Well, maybe I'm exaggerating."

"You certainly are, and this forest is no more mysterious than your great woods of the Far West! . . . We haven't even to fear an attack by the Redskins! . . . Here there are none of those ferocious tribes who infest the regions of the north-east, clamouring for meat like the regular cannibals which they've never stopped being! . . . No, and this water course which we've named after Dr. Johausen, whose trail I so much wanted to discover, this rio, so quiet and reliable, will lead us to the Oubanghi without any trouble . . ."

"The Oubanghi, my dear Max, which we should equally have reached by going around the forest, by

JULES VERNE

following the route mapped out by poor old Urdax, and that in a comfortable wagon where we'd have wanted for nothing until the journey ended!"

"You're quite right, John, and that certainly would have been better! . . . Certainly this forest is quite commonplace and doesn't deserve to be visited! . . . It's only a wood, a big wood, nothing else! . . . And yet at the start it aroused my curiosity . . . You recollect those flames which lit up the clearing, those torches which shone through the branches of its foremost trees! . . . Then . . . Nobody! . . . Where the devil can those Negroes have got to! . . . I find myself looking for them at times amidst these giant trees! . . . No . . . not one human being . . ."

"Max!" John Cort interrupted him.

"John?" Max Huber replied.

"Will you look in that direction . . . downstream, on the left bank?"

"What? . . . a native?"

"Yes . . . but a native with four legs! . . . Down there, above the reeds, a splendid pair of horns curving backwards . . ."

The foreloper's attention had been attracted. "A buffalo," he said.

"A buffalo!" Max Huber repeated as he seized his carbine. "That's a splendid main dish and if I can get it within range . . ."

Khamis gave a vigorous thrust on the steering-oar, and the raft made obliquely to the bank. A few minutes later it was only thirty yards away.

"What a prospect of beef-steaks!" Max Huber murmured, his carbine supported on his left knee.

"You can have the first shot, Max," John Cort told him, "and I'll have the second . . . if we need it . . ."

The buffalo did not seem inclined to leave its position. Stopped down-wind, it was hardly sniffing the air, and it had not the slightest suspicion of the danger it was running. As nobody could take aim at its heart

THE VILLAGE IN THE TREETOPS

they would have to fire at its head, and that was what Max Huber did as soon as he got it under his sights.

The explosion rang out, the animal's tail was contorted above the reeds, a pain-stricken roar arose through space—not the usual bellow but a proof that it had received a mortal blow.

"That's got him!" In his excitement Max Huber used rather a colloquial expression.

There was certainly no need for John Cort to second his efforts, and this saved another cartridge. Falling among the reeds, the animal slid down to the foot of the bank, emitting a jet of blood which reddened the clear water of the Rio Johausen.

So as not to lose this splendid quarry, the raft was steered towards the place where the animal had fallen, and the foreloper got ready to cut it up on the spot so as to take its best portions away.

The two friends could not but admire this specimen of the wild bulls of Africa, of gigantic size. When these animals cross the plains in herds of two or three hundred, it may well be imagined how furiously they gallop and what clouds of dust they raise!

It was an onja, to use the name given them by the natives, a solitary bull, larger than its fellows of Europe, its forehead narrower, its muzzle longer, its horns more compressed. Max Huber had certainly been lucky. If an onja does not fall at the first shot it is terrible when it hurls itself upon the hunter.

Using his axe and knife, Khamis began to cut the beast up, an operation in which his companions helped him as best they could. It was essential not to overload the raft, and forty pounds of this appetising flesh would supply enough food for several days.

But while this task was going on Llanga, usually so inquisitive about whatever interested his friends Max and John, had stayed under the shelter, and for the following reason:

At the sound of the explosion the little creature had

JULES VERNE

been aroused. Its arms had moved slightly. If its eyelids had not been raised, at least from its half-open mouth, from its pallid lips, there had once again come the one word which Llanga had previously heard:

"Ngora! Ngora!"

This time Llanga could not be mistaken. The word reached his ears with a strange articulation and a sort of rolling of the letter "R."

Touched by the pitiful tones of this poor creature, Llanga took its hand, burning with a fever which had lasted since the previous evening. He filled his cup with fresh water and tried unsuccessfully to pour a few drops into the tightly-closed mouth. The jaws, whose teeth were dazzling white, did not open. So Llanga, moistening a turf of dry grass, gently washed the lips. That seemed to do the poor creature a little good. Its hand feebly pressed his and once again it uttered the word *"Ngora."*

And it must not be forgotten that this word, of Congolese origin, is the one which the natives use to speak of their mother. So was the little creature really calling for its own parent?

Llanga's sympathy was increased by a quite natural pity as he reflected that this word might perhaps be lost in the creature's last sigh! . . . A monkey? . . . That was what Max Huber had said. No, this was not a monkey! . . . Here was something that Llanga, with his limited intelligence, could not possibly explain.

He stayed there for an hour, sometimes stroking the hand of his protégé, sometimes moistening its lips, and he did not leave it until it had again fallen into sleep. Then Llanga, making up his mind to say everything, went to join his friends, while the raft, thrust off from the bank, had gone back into the current.

"Well," smiled Max Huber, "how's your monkey getting on?"

Llanga looked at him as if hesitating to speak. Then,

THE VILLAGE IN THE TREETOPS

putting his hand on his friend's arm, he replied, "It isn't a monkey."

"Not a monkey?" John Cort repeated.

"Well, he's an obstinate one, our Llanga is!" exclaimed Max Huber. "Look here! You've got it into your head that it's a child like yourself?"

"A child . . . not like me . . . but a child . . ."

"Listen, Llanga," John Cort continued more seriously than his companions, "You're trying to make out it's a child."

"Yes . . . it spoke . . . that night . . ."

"It spoke?"

"And it's just spoken now . . ."

"And what did the little prodigy say?" asked Max Huber.

"It said '*Ngora*' . . ."

"What! . . . that word I heard myself?" John Cort could not conceal his surprise.

"Yes . . . '*Ngora*,' " the young native declared.

There were only two possibilities: either Llanga had been the victim of some illusion, or he had lost his head.

"Let's verify that," John Cort suggested, "and so long as it's true, that at least will be something out of the ordinary, my dear Max!"

They went into the shelter and examined the little creature.

At first sight it certainly seemed to belong to the simian race. But what at once struck John Cort was that he was confronted not with a four-handed but with a two-handed creature. And it is generally agreed that man alone belongs to that order in the animal kingdom. This strange creature possessed only two hands, while the monkeys, without exception, have four; moreover its feet conformed to the walking type and were not prehensile like those of the simians.

He pointed this out to Max Huber.

"Strange . . . very strange!" replied the latter.

The size of this little creature did not exceed a couple

of feet. It seemed to be in its infancy and could not be more than five or six years old. It skin, devoid of any fur, was covered with a light russet down. On its forehead, its chin, its cheeks, there were no hairs; these grew only on its chest, its thighs, and its arms. It ears ended in soft rounded flesh, very different from those of the apes which have no lobes. It arms were not very long. Nature had not endowed it with the fifth member, common to most of the monkeys, that tail which they use for feeling and gripping. Its head was rounded, its facial angle about forty-five degrees, its nose flattened, its forehead not receding. If there were no hairs on its head, there was at any rate a sort of wool similar to that of the natives of Central Africa. This creature certainly took more after men than after monkeys in its general appearance, and probably too in its internal organisation.

The astonishment felt by Max Huber and John Cort may well be imagined. Here they were in the presence of a creature absolutely new, which no anthrolpologist had so far observed, and which on the whole seemed to be mid-way between the animals and man.

And then Llanga had declared that it had spoken—provided that the young native had not mistaken for an articulated word what was merely a cry not corresponding to any idea, a cry due not to intelligence but to instinct.

The two friends stayed silent, hoping that the little creature's mouth would open, while Llanga went on moistening its forehead and temples. But its respiration was less panting, its skin less hot; its attack of fever was coming to an end. At last it lips parted slightly.

"*Ngora ... Ngora! ...*" it repeated.

"Well," exclaimed Max Huber, "here's something which goes beyond all reason."

Neither of the two men wanted to believe what they had just heard.

What! This creature, whatever it was, which certainly

THE VILLAGE IN THE TREETOPS

did not occupy a high rung on the ladder of animal life, possessed the gift of speech! ... Though it had only pronounced this one word of the Congolese language, might they not suppose that it used others, that it had ideas, that it knew how to put them into sentences? ...

What was to be regretted that was its eyes had not opened, and that the men could not seek in them that expression which denotes thought and which is responsive to as much. No, its eyelids were still closed and nothing indicated that they were going to open. ...

John Cort had bent over the creature, so that no words or cries could escape him. He supported its head without waking it, and what was his surprise when he saw a cord tied round that little neck.

He slid that cord round—it was made of a skein of silk—so as to reach the knot which held it; then suddenly he exclaimed, "A medal!"

"A medal?" Max Huber repeated.

John Cort untied the cord.

Yes, a medal of nickel, the size of a halfpenny, with a name engraved on one side and a portrait on the other.

The name was that of Johausen and the portrait was that of the doctor.

"Him!" exclaimed Max Huber, "and here's this urchin decorated with the Order of the German Professor, the one whose empty cage we found!"

There was nothing astonishing in these medals having spread into the Cameroons, for Dr. Johausen had often distributed them among the people of the Congo. But that an emblem of this kind should be tied, of all places, to the neck of this strange inhabitant of the Oubanghi forest ...

"It's fantastic," declared Max Huber, "so long as these monkey-men haven't stolen this medal from the doctor's strongbox ..."

"Khamis?" John Cort was calling the foreloper to tell him about these extraordinary happenings and to ask him what he thought of them.

JULES VERNE

But at that moment the foreloper's voice could be heard crying, "Mr. Max . . . Mr. John!"

The two men left the shelter and went up to him.

"Listen," he told them.

About five hundred yards downstream the river was swerving sharply to the right at a bend where the trees had reappeared in thick clusters. Stretched in that direction, the ear could detect a dull continuous roaring, which did not in any way resemble the bellowing of animals or the howls of wild beasts. It was a sort of uproar which kept increasing the further the raft went downstream . . .

"A strange sound . . ." said John Cort.

"And I can't recognise it," added Max Huber.

"Perhaps there's a fall or a rapid down there?" the foreloper suggested. "The wind's blowing from the south and I can feel that the air's getting damp!"

Khamis was not mistaken. Over the surface of the rio was passing a sort of liquid vapor which could be produced only by a violent disturbance of the waters.

If the river were barred by any obstacle, if navigation were to be interrupted, that would be a serious development which Max Huber and John Cort had no more suspected than had Llanga and his *protégé*.

The raft was drifting downstream with some speed, and as soon as it got beyond the bend they would know the cause of that distant tumult. When it had been passed the foreloper's fears proved only too well-founded.

At a distance of about a hundred fathoms a pile of blackish rocks dammed the river from side to side, except at its mid-point, through which the foam-crowned waters were rushing. On each side they had come up against a natural dyke and in some places they were flowing over it. Thus there was a rapid in mid-stream with waterfalls on its two sides.

If the raft did not succeed in gaining one of the banks, if they could not secure it firmly, it would be carried

THE VILLAGE IN THE TREETOPS

away and smashed against the dam—unless of course it capsized in the rapids.

Though they were quite cool, the men realised that there was not an instant to lose; the current was getting swifter.

"Make for the bank . . . for the bank!" shouted Khamis.

It was then half past six and in that misty weather the twilight left only a doubtful gleam which scarcely allowed anything to be distinguished. This difficulty, on top of so many others, made handling the raft even more complicated.

It was in vain that Khamis tried to steer towards the bank: he was not strong enough. Max Huber joined him in an attempt to resist the current, which was carrying them straight towards the center of the dam. Together they would have managed it, they would have succeeded in getting out of the current—if the steering oar had not snapped.

"Be ready to jump on to the rocks before we get swept into the rapids," Khamis told them.

"There's nothing else to do!" John Cort agreed.

The noise had brought Llanga from under the shelter, and at a glance he realised the danger. Instead of thinking of himself he remembered somebody else, the child. He went and caught it up in his arms and knelt down in the stern.

A minute later, and the raft was once more caught by the rapids. But perhaps it would not be swept up against the dam and it might be through the gap without capsizing? . . .

A stroke of bad luck swept it aside, and it was against one of the rocks on the left side of the dam that the fragile contraption was hurled with extreme violence. In vain Khamis and his companions tried to hang on to the dam, on which they were able to throw the box of cartridges, the weapons, the tools . . .

They were all hurled into the whirlpool just at the very instant when the raft was smashed. Its fragments vanished downstream in the midst of the roaring waters.

CHAPTER XII

BENEATH THE TREES

NEXT DAY three men were stretched out near a fire whose last cinders were just being consumed. Overcome by fatigue, incapable of resisting their weariness, the men, after spreading their clothing to dry before the fire, had fallen asleep.

What time was it and was it day or night? . . . None of them would have been able to say. However, by calculating the time which had elapsed since the previous evening, it seemed that the sun must be above the horizon. But in which direction was east? . . . This question, if it had been asked, would have remained unanswered.

Were these three men in the depths of a cave, in some place where the light of day could not penetrate? . . .

No, but around them the trees were so thick that they cut off the view at a distance of several yards. Even when the fire was burning it would have been impossible to find a practicable footpath between those enormous trunks and the lianas which bound them together. The lower branches formed a platform only about fifty feet from the ground, and so dense was the foliage above, right up to the tops of the trees, that neither the gleam of the stars nor the glare of the sun could pass through them. A prison would have been no

THE VILLAGE IN THE TREETOPS

darker, its walls would have been no more impenetrable, and yet this was only one of the masses of undergrowth of the great forest.

In those three men might have been recognised John Cort, Max Huber, and Khamis.

What chain of circumstances had brought them here? ... They did not know. After the raft had been smashed against the dam, they had been unable to hang on to the rocks, they had been hurled into the waters of the rapids, and they knew nothing of what had followed the catastrophe. To whom did the foreloper and his comrades owe their salvation? ... Who had carried them into this thick undergrowth before they had regained consciousness? ...

Unfortunately they had not all escaped from the disaster. One of them was missing, the adopted child of John Cort and Max Huber, the poor Llanga, and with him the little creature which he had saved once ... And who knew whether it were not in trying to save it a second time that he had perished with it? ...

Now the three men possessed neither ammunition nor arms; nor did they have any tools except for their knives and the axe which the foreloper carried in his belt. There was no raft, and on what side were they to look to return to the course of the Rio Johausen? ...

And the question of food, how was that to be answered? Presumably they could get nothing by hunting? ... So, the three men would be reduced to roots, to wild fruits, an insufficient resource and one which, what was more, was problematical? ... Were they not likely, after a short respite, to die of hunger? ...

A respite of two or three days, anyhow, for at least food was assured to them for that length of time. The remains of the buffalo had been placed beside them. After having shared a few slices, which were already cooked, they had fallen asleep around that fire which was just on the verge of going out.

John Cort was the first to awake in the midst of a

JULES VERNE

darkness which night would not have made more complete. As his eyes grew accustomed to the dimness he vaguely saw Max Huber and Khamis lying at the foot of the trees. Before arousing them from slumber, he went to rekindle the fire by pulling together the odds and ends of wood which were burning beneath the ashes. Then he picked up an armful of dead wood and dry grass, and soon a crackling flame was throwing its gleam on the camp.

"Now," said John Cort, "let's think about getting out of it! . . ."

The crackling of the flames soon aroused Max Huber and Khamis, who jumped up almost at the same moment. Realisation of their position returned to them and they had to decide what would be best to do: they held an informal council.

"Where are we? . . ." asked Max Huber.

"Where someone's carried us," replied John Cort, "and by that I mean that we don't know what's happened for the last . . ."

"For the last night and day, perhaps," Max Huber completed the sentence for him. "Was it yesterday that our raft was smashed against the dam? . . . Khamis, have you any ideas about it?"

The foreloper's only response was to shake his head. It was impossible to judge the time which had elapsed or to say in what conditions their rescue had been carried out.

"And Llanga?" asked John Cort, "he must have perished, for he isn't with us now! . . . The people who saved us couldn't have dragged him out of the rapids . . ."

"Poor child!" Max Huber sighed, "he was so very fond of us! . . . We liked him so much . . . We'd have made his life so happy! . . . To have saved him from the hands of those Denkas, and now . . . poor child!"

The two friends would not have hesitated to risk their lives for Llanga . . . but they too had come near to

THE VILLAGE IN THE TREETOPS

perishing in the whirlpool, nor did they know who had saved them . . .

It need hardly be added that they spared no thought to the strange creature which the young native had picked up and which no doubt had perished with him. They had plenty of other things to occupy their minds—questions much more serious than this anthropological problem regarding some creature that was half human and half ape.

"When I think it over," John Cort continued, "I can't recall anything that happened after we collided with the dam . . . ! A little before that, I thought I saw Khamis standing up and throwing the weapons and tools on to the rocks . . ."

"Yes," said Khamis, "and fortunately they didn't fall into the river . . . Then . . ."

"Then," Max Huber declared, "just as we'd been swallowed up, I thought . . . yes . . . I thought I could see some men . . ."

"Some men . . . certainly . . ." replied John Cort. "Natives who were gesticulating and yelling and hurling themselves towards the dam . . ."

"You saw those natives?" The foreloper was astonished.

"About a dozen," Max Huber assured him, "and they were probably the ones who dragged us out of the rio . . ."

"Then," John Cort added, "without waiting for us to regain consciousness they must have carried us here . . . with the remains of our food . . . Then, having kindled that fire, they vanished hastily . . ."

"And they vanished so completely," added Max Huber, "that we can't find any trace of them! . . . That's to show how little they value our gratitude . . ."

"Patience, my dear Max," John Cort advised him, "it's just possible that they're somewhere around the camp . . . Can we suppose that they brought us here simply to forsake us? . . ."

"And in what a place!" Max Huber exclaimed. "That

there could be in this Oubanghi forest so thick an undergrowth, that passes the imagination! . . . We're in complete darkness . . ."

"Agreed. But is it daytime!" John replied.

This question was soon answered in the affirmative. Opaque though the foliage was, they could see, above the tops of the trees a hundred or a hundred and fifty feet high, vague gleams of space. It could not be doubted that at the very moment the sky was lighting up the horizon. The watches of the two men, plunged into the waters of the river, no longer showed the time. So they would have to depend on the position of the sun, and yet it might not be possible for its rays to penetrate through the branches.

While the two friends were raising questions to which they did not know how to reply, Khamis was listening to them without saying a word. He had got up, he was walking up and down along the narrow space which the enormous trees had left free, surrounded as it was by a barrier of lianas and thorns. At the same time he was trying to find some glimpse of sky between the branches; to regain that sense of direction for which he had never had so great a need. Though he had many times explored the woods of the Congo and the Cameroons he had never come across regions so impenetrable. This part of the great forest could not be compared to those which he and his companions had crossed before reaching the Rio Johausen. From then on they had generally made for the south-west. But in what direction was the south-west, and would his instinct be enough for him to find out? . . .

Just as John Cort, guessing the reason for his hesitation, was going to question him, it was the foreloper who spoke first: "Mr. Max, you're certain you saw natives close to the dam?"

"Quite certain, Khamis, just at the moment when the raft was crashing against the rocks."

"And on which of the banks?"

THE VILLAGE IN THE TREETOPS

"On the left bank."

"You're sure it was the left bank?"

"Yes . . . the left bank."

"So we must be to the east of the stream?"

"Doubtless, and so," John Cort added, "in the thickest part of the forest . . . But how far are we from the rio? . . ."

"The distance can't be very great," Max Huber declared, "to estimate it at a couple of miles, that would be to exaggerate . . . We can't think that our rescuers, whoever they may be, could have carried us far . . ."

"That's my opinion too," Khamis agreed, "the river can't be far away . . . So it would be best for us to go back to it so as to start sailing below the dam as soon as we've built a raft . . ."

"And how can we live until then, or while we're going down to the Oubanghi? . . ." Max Huber objected, "we haven't anything to hunt with . . ."

"What's more," asked John Cort, "on which side are we to look for the stream? That we landed on the left bank, I quite agree . . . But seeing how impossible it is to get our direction, can we say that the rio is on one side of us rather than on the other?"

"And first of all," Max Huber wanted to know, "in which way, if you please, are we to get out of this undergrowth?"

"This way," the foreloper replied. And he showed a gap in the curtain of lianas through which he and his companions must have been brought into this clearing. Beyond was a dark winding footpath which looked quite practicable.

Where did that footpath lead? . . . Was it to the Rio Johausen? . . . Nothing could be less certain . . . Might it not intermingle with others? . . . Might they not risk getting lost in that maze? . . . Anyhow, within two days the remains of the buffalo would have been eaten . . . And afterwards? . . . As for quenching their thirst, the rains came frequently enough to remove all fears on that score.

"In any case," commented John Cort, "it isn't by taking root here that we'll get out of our difficulties, and we must clear out of this as soon as we can."

"Let's eat first," suggested Max Huber.

About two pounds of meat was divided into three portions and each of them had to be content with that scanty meal! . . .

"And to think," Max Huber continued, "that we don't even know whether it's lunch or dinner . . ."

"What does that matter!" John Cort replied, "our stomachs don't care . . ."

"Yes, but our stomachs need to drink and I'd welcome a few drops of the Rio Johausen like the finest of the vintage wines of France!"

While they were eating they fell silent. From the surrounding darkness came a vague impression of disquiet and anxiety. The air, filled with the smell of the damp ground, was heavy under that dome of foliage. And in that place, which seemed unsuited even for the flight of birds, not a cry, not a song, not the flutter of a wing. Sometimes the dry noise of a dead branch whose fall was muffled by contact with the carpet of spongy moss which stretched from trunk to trunk. Occasionally too, a shrill hiss, and then the rustle between the dry leaves of a snake, about a foot long and fortunately quite harmless. As for the insects, they buzzed as usual and were not sparing of their stings.

The meal finished, the three men got up.

After picking up the remains of the buffalo, Khamis made for the passage which led between the lianas.

Time and again and at the top of his voice, Max Huber shouted, "Llanga! . . . Llanga! . . . Llanga! . . ."

It was in vain, and not even an echo sent back the name of the little native.

"Let's get away," and the foreloper went ahead.

THE VILLAGE IN THE TREETOPS

Scarcely had he set his foot on the path when he exclaimed:

"A light!"

Max Huber and John Cort hurried towards him.

"Natives?" one of them suggested.

"Let's wait," replied the other.

The light—probably a burning torch—appeared down the footpath several hundred paces away. It lit up the depths of the wood but feebly, throwing a livid gleam on the underside of the high branches.

Whoever carried it, where was he going? . . . Was he alone? . . . Did they have to fear an attack, or was help coming to them? . . .

Khamis and the two friends hesitated before going further into the forest. Two or three minutes elapsed. The torch had not moved.

As for thinking that this gleam was that of a will-o'-the-wisp, its immobility put that out of the question.

"What are we to do?" asked John Cort.

"Make for that light, as it isn't coming to us," Max Huber replied.

"Let's get on," Khamis advised them.

He went a few paces down the footpath. At once the torch began to move away. Had whoever carried it noticed that the three strangers were beginning to move? . . . Did he want to light up their way under these dark clumps and to lead them towards the Rio Johausen or some other tributary of the Oubanghi? . . . This was not a time for hanging about. First they had to follow that light and then to try to make their way once more towards the south-west.

So here they were, following the narrow path, over a soil whose grass had long been trodden down, the lianas broken, the bushes crushed, by animals or by man.

The three men walked on for about three hours; when they stopped to take breath, the light stopped at the same moment . . .

"Certainly it's a guide," Max Huber declared, "a guide who's being very obliging! . . . If only we knew where he's taking us . . ."

"So long as he takes us out of this maze," John Cort replied, "I won't ask anything more! . . . Well, Max, isn't this quite extraordinary enough for you?"

"Quite enough, to be sure!"

"So long as it doesn't get too extraordinary, my friend," John Cort added.

Throughout the afternoon the winding footpath never stopped traversing a foliage which became more and more opaque. Khamis went ahead with his companions behind him, in Indian file, for the path was only wide enough for one person. If they hurried on in the hope of catching up their guide, he likewise increased his pace, invariably keeping the same distance.

By six in the evening, they calculated, four or five leagues had been crossed since they set out. It was the intention of Khamis, in spite of his fatigue, to follow that light so long as it showed itself, and he was going to get on the move again when suddenly it went out.

"Let's stop," John Cort suggested, "that's clearly a hint for us to . . ."

"Or rather it's an order," commented Max Huber.

"Let's obey it anyhow," the foreloper replied, "and let's spend the night here."

"But tomorrow," John Cort added, "will the light be visible again?"

That was the question. The three of them stretched themselves out at the foot of a tree. They shared a fragment of buffalo meat, and fortunately they could quench their thirst at a trickle of water which wound through the grass. Although the rains were very frequent in the forest, not a drop had fallen for forty-eight hours.

"Who knows," asked John Cort, "if our guide hasn't chosen this place simply so that we could get something to drink?"

"Very thoughtful of him," Max Huber declared, as he

THE VILLAGE IN THE TREETOPS

lifted a little of that cool water in a leaf rolled up into a cone.

However disquieting their position might be, weariness overcame them and sleep could no longer wait. But the two friends did not fall asleep without having remembered Llanga . . . The poor child! . . . Had he been drowned in the rapids? . . . If he had been saved, why hadn't they seen him? . . . Why hadn't he come to join his two friends, John and Max? . . .

When they awoke a gleam of light, penetrating between the branches, showed that it was daylight. Khamis was able to infer that they had been going eastwards. Unfortunately, this was the wrong way . . . Anyhow, all they could do was to push on.

No adventure marked 22nd March. The burning torch never stopped guiding them, always towards the east.

On each side of the footpath the undergrowth seemed impenetrable, the tree-trunks growing closely together amid an inextricable tangle of bushes. The foreloper and his comrades seemed to be making their way through an endless tunnel of foliage.

They had not seen any animal, and indeed, how could any creature of any size have got so far? There were no more of those trails which the foreloper had taken advantage of before reaching the banks of the Rio Johausen.

Even if the two hunters had had their guns, how useless these would have been, for there was not the slightest vestige of any game.

So it was with well-justified apprehension that the three men saw that their food had almost completely given out.

As on the previous day the torch went out towards evening: and, as on the preceding night, they had nothing to disturb their rest.

When John Cort was first to wake up, he aroused his companions with a shout.

"Somebody's been here while we were asleep!"

JULES VERNE

And indeed a fire had been kindled, a number of cinders were glowing and a piece of antelope meat was hanging from one of the low branches of an acacia above a tiny stream. Max Huber did not utter an exclamation of surprise. Neither he nor his companions wanted to discuss the strangeness of their situation, this unknown guide who was leading them towards a goal no less unknown, this spirit of the great forest whose tracks they had been following for two days! . . .

As hunger was making itself felt, Khamis grilled the piece of antelope meat. This would suffice for both meals, at noon and in the evening.

Then the torch gave the signal to start.

Their progress continued in the same conditions. During the afternoon, however, they realised that the undergrowth was gradually becoming less dense. The daylight was coming into it more clearly, at least between the treetops. Yet it was still impossible to make out whoever it was who was preceding them. Just as before, five or six leagues were traversed that day, and they must have gone about forty miles since leaving the Rio Johausen.

That evening, just as the torch went out, the three men stopped. It must be night, for complete darkness surrounded the trees.

Wearied out by their long march, after having finished their meat and quenched their thirst with fresh water, they stretched themselves out at the foot of the tree and fell asleep. And—but surely this was in a dream—could Max Huber hear the sound of some instrument which somewhere above his head was playing the Waltz from Weber's *Freyschütz!*

THE VILLAGE IN THE TREETOPS

CHAPTER XIII

THE VILLAGE IN THE TREETOPS

NEXT DAY when they awoke the men noticed, not without great surprise, that the darkness was more complete than ever in that part of the forest. Was it daytime? . . . They could not be certain. Anyhow, the light which had guided them for over sixty hours had not reappeared. So they would have to wait until it showed itself before they could resume their progress. From a comment made by John Cort could be deduced certain consequences.

"What we've got to notice," he said, "is that we haven't got any fire this morning and that nobody's come during the night to bring us our grub . . ."

"What's worse still," Max Huber added, "is that we've got nothing left."

"Perhaps," the foreloper suggested, "that shows that we've got there . . ."

"Where?" asked John Cort.

"Where they're taking us, my dear John!"

This was a reply which did not reply to anything; but how could anyone have been more explicit? . . .

Something else to be noticed: if the forest were darker it did not seem to be more silent. They could hear a sort of buzzing in the treetops, a vague noise which came from the branches above. Looking upwards, the three men could vaguely see something like a great platform stretched out about a hundred feet above the ground.

There must doubtless be at that height a tremendous entanglement of branches without any cranny through which the daylight could pierce. A thatched roof would not have been more light-proof. This explained the darkness which prevailed beneath the trees.

JULES VERNE

Where they had camped that night the nature of the ground had changed greatly. No more intermingled brambles, no more of these thorns which had kept them from leaving the footpath. A scanty grass, like a prairie which neither rain nor spring ever watered. The trees, at intervals of twenty to thirty feet, resembled pillars supporting some colossal edifice, and their branches must cover an area of several thousand square yards.

There were indeed masses of African sycamores whose trunks were formed of a number of stems firmly united together; baobabs, recognisable by the gourd-like shape of their base, with a circumference of twenty to thirty yards and surmounted by an enormous mass of hanging branches; palm trees with forked trunks; silk cotton trees with their trunks opening into a series of hollows big enough for a man to hide in; mahogany trees with trunks a yard and a half in diameter from which might have been excavated dug-out canoes from fifteen to eighteen yards long and able to carry three or four tons.

About an hour elapsed. Khamis never stopped looking from side to side, searching for the light which had guided them . . . And yet he had wanted to give up following that guide? . . . To tell the truth his instinct, combined with certain observations he had made, inclined him to think that they had still been going eastwards, and it was not on that side that the Oubanghi was flowing nor was this the way back . . . So where had that strange light led them? . . .

If it did not show itself again, what were they to do? . . . To leave that place? . . . But to go where? . . . To stay where? . . . And how would they provide for themselves on their way? . . . Already they were hungry and thirsty . . .

"Anyhow," said John Cort, "we shall certainly have to start, and I'm wondering whether it wouldn't be better to get off at once?"

"In what direction?" Max Huber objected.

THE VILLAGE IN THE TREETOPS

That was the question, and what clue could they rely on to solve it? . . .

"Well," John Cort was getting impatient, "we aren't short of legs, so far as I know! . . . It's possible to get between these trees, and it isn't too dark for us to find our way . . ."

"Come on," said Khamis.

The three of them went to explore the country for about a quarter of a mile around. Everywhere they trod on the same ground devoid of any trees, the same bare dry carpet, as if they had been under the shelter of a roof as impenetrable to the rain as to the rays of the sun. Everywhere the same trees, only their lower branches being visible. And always that same vague noise which seemed to be coming from above and whose origin was still inexplicable. Was this part of the forest completely deserted? . . . No, and more than once Khamis thought he could see shadows moving between the trees. Was this an illusion? . . . He did not know what to think. At last, after half an hour of fruitless effort, he and his companions sat down at the foot of a tree.

Their eyes were getting used to this darkness, which was moreover diminishing. Thanks to the rising sun, a little daylight was spreading beneath that platform which sheltered the ground. Already they could distinguish objects a score of paces away.

"Something's moving down there . . ." the foreloper muttered.

"An animal or a man?" asked John Cort, looking in that direction.

"It must be a child, anyhow," Khamis pointed out, "because it's so small . . ."

"A monkey!" Max Huber declared.

They kept silent and motionless so as not to frighten the ape. If they should succeed in getting hold of it, then, in spite of the repugnance which Max Huber and John Cort showed to monkey-flesh . . . But, indeed, lacking a fire, how would the grill or roast it? . . .

JULES VERNE

Although it was approaching, the creature did not show any signs of astonishment. It was walking on its hind legs and it stopped a few paces away. What was the surprise of John Cort and Max Huber when they recognised the creature which Llanga had saved and adopted! ... They exchanged a few words:

"It ... that's it ..."

"To be sure it is ..."

"But then, as it's here, why isn't Llanga here? ..."

"Are you sure you're not mistaken?" asked the foreloper.

"Quite sure," John Cort declared, "and anyhow, we'll soon find out!"

He took the medal from his pocket and, holding it by its cord, he swung it before the little creature's eyes to attract it.

Scarcely had the infant seen that medal than he leaped forward. He certainly wasn't ill now! ... During the three days which had elapsed he had regained his health as well as his natural agility. He jumped towards John Cort with the plain intention of regaining his property. Khamis seized him as he moved and now it was not the word "*Ngora*" which escaped from the mouth of the little creature, it was these words clearly articulated:

"*Li-maï ... Ngala ... Ngala!* ..."

What was the meaning of these words in a language unknown even to Khamis, neither he nor his companions had time to ask. There suddenly appeared other creatures of the same species, but taller, being not less than five feet and a half from head to toe. The three travellers could not even make out whether they were dealing with men or with apes. To resist these woodland creatures of the great forest, a score or so in number, would have been useless. The men were gripped by the arms, thrust forward, made to go beneath the trees, and surrounded as they were they did not stop until after they had gone several hundred yards.

THE VILLAGE IN THE TREETOPS

There, two trees, fairly close together, sloped in such a way as to allow cross-branches to be fixed to them, step-fashion. If it was not a stairway, it was better than a ladder. Five or six individuals of the escort climbed up it, while the others forced their prisoners to follow in the same way, without however ill-using them.

The higher they got the clearer they could see the light through the foliage. Between the gaps came several rays of that sunlight of which the three men had been deprived since they had left the river.

Max Huber would not have been in good faith if he had refused to agree that this certainly came under the heading of something extraordinary.

When the climb ended a hundred or so feet above the ground, what was their surprise: before them stretched a platform lit up by the light of the sky. Above it were the leafy tops of the trees. On its surface were arranged in a certain order huts of yellow clay and foliage bordering some streets. The whole formed a village built at this height on an expanse whose limits could not be seen.

Here were coming and going a crowd of natives of a species similar to that of Llanga's *protégé*. Their posture, similar to that of man, showed that they were in the habit of walking upright. Thus they had a right to the term *erectus* given by Doctor Eugene Dubois to the *pithecanthropus* found in the forests of Java—an anthropological character which the savant regarded as one of the most important of the intermediaries between man and the monkeys postulated by Darwin.*

---

*It was in the Lower Quaternary of Sumatra that Dr. E. Dubois, a Dutch military doctor at Batavia, had found a skull, a thighbone, and a tooth in a good state of preservation. The size of the cranial cavity being much greater than that of the largest gorilla but smaller than that of man, this creature really appeared to be an intermediary between the ape and man. —J.V.

But Khamis, Max Huber and John Cort had to defer until later their observations on this subject. Whether these beings ought or ought not to be placed between the animal and man, their escort, while talking in some incomprehensible language, pushed them into a hut in the midst of a population which looked at them without seeming much astonished. The door was closed upon them, and there they were well and truly imprisoned in the said hut.

"Perfect!" Max Huber declared, "and what surprises me most is that these fellows don't seem to have an air of paying us any attention! . . . Have they seen men before? . . ."

"That's quite possible," replied John Cort, "but it remains to be seen whether they're in the habit of feeding their prisoners . . ."

"Or whether they don't feed upon them!" added Max Huber.

Anyhow, that these creatures were anthropoids of a higher species than the orangs of Borneo, the chimpanzees of Guinea, the gorillas of Gaboon, which are nearest to humanity—that could not be doubted. They certainly knew how to make fire and had several other domestic conveniences. Among these was the hearth at the first camp and the torch which their guide had carried through the lonely darkness. And the idea at once leaped to the mind that those moving flames which had been seen at the edge of the forest had been kindled by these strange creatures who inhabited it. What it was also necessary to note was that these creatures, of unknown species, were built like human beings for standing and walking. No other ape would have been more worthy to share the name of Orang, the exact meaning of which is "Man of the Woods."

"And what's more, they talk," commented John Cort, after several remarks had been exchanged on the subject of these inhabitants of this village in the treetops.

"Well, if they speak," replied Max Huber, "they must

THE VILLAGE IN THE TREETOPS

have words to express themselves, especially those which say: 'I'm dying of hunger! ... when do we sit down to a meal?' ... I shouldn't be sorry to know them!"

There are prisoners who resign themselves to their captivity and others who do not. John Cort and the foreloper—and especially the impatient Max Huber—did not belong to the former category. Besides the annoyance of being shut up in the depths of this hut and the impossibility of seeing anything through its walls, their uncertainty as to the future and as to the outcome of this adventure was quite enough to preoccupy them. And then hunger was making itself felt, their last meal having been consumed fifteen hours before. There was however one circumstance on which could be based a hope, admittedly vague: it was that Llanga's *protégé* dwelt in this village—probably his birthplace—and in the midst of his family, granted that what one calls the family existed among these forest-dwellers of the Oubanghi.

"So," said John Cort, "because that little fellow was saved from the whirlpool we can be permitted to think that Llanga was too ... They'd never have left one another, and if Llanga learned that three men had just been brought into the village, how could he fail to realise that they were ourselves? ... On the whole nobody has done us any harm so far and its probable that they haven't hurt Llanga ..."

"Certainly the *protégé* is safe and sound," Max Huber conceded. "But what about the protector? ... Nothing to show that our poor Llanga hasn't perished in the rio!"

Nothing, indeed. But at that moment the door of the hut, which was guarded by two strong-looking fellows, opened, and the young native appeared.

"Llanga ... Llanga!" the two friends cried at once.

"My friend Max ... my friend John!" replied Llanga as he fell into their arms.

"How long have you been here?" the foreloper asked.

JULES VERNE

"Since yesterday morning."

"And how did you get here?"

"Somebody carried me through the forest."

"The ones who carried you must have walked quicker than we did, Llanga?"

"Very quickly!"

"And who was it who carried you?"

"One of those who saved me . . . and who saved you too."

"Men?"

"Yes . . . men . . . not monkeys . . . no, not monkeys!"

The young native was still very definite. Anyhow, these were examples of some special race no doubt subject to the word "less" compared with humanity . . . An intermediate race of primitive people, perhaps examples of those anthropopithecoids who are missing in the animal scale . . .

Then Llanga briefly related his history, but not before he had several times kissed the hands of the Frenchman and the American who had been pulled like himself from the rapids and whom he had never hoped to see again. When the raft had hit against the rock, they had hurled themselves into the torrent, he and Li-maï . . .

"Li-Maï?" exclaimed Max Huber.

"Yes . . . Li-Maï . . . that's his name . . . he repeated it and kept pointing to himself. "Li-Maï . . . Li-Maï."

"So he's got a name?" asked John Cort.

"Certainly, John! . . . when people can speak isn't it natural for them to give themselves a name? . . ."

"And does this tribe, this people, whatever you like to call it," asked John Cort, "give itself a name too?"

"Yes . . . the Waggdis . . ." replied Llanga, "I heard Li-Maï call them Waggdis!"

This word certainly did not belong to the Congolese language. But, Waggdis or otherwise, these natives had happened to be on the left bank of the Rio Johausen when the catastrophe took place. Some of them had run

THE VILLAGE IN THE TREETOPS

along the dam and plunged into the torrent to rescue the three men, the others to save Li-Maï and Llanga. The latter, having lost consciousness, could not remember any more of what had happened next and had believed that his friends had been drowned in the river.

When Llanga returned to himself he was in the arms of a robust Waggdi, the father of Li-Maï, who himself was in the arms of the *"Ngora"* his mother! What could be assumed was that a few days before he had met Llanga, the little creature had got lost in the forest and that his parents had gone to look for him. It is already clear how Llanga had saved him, how, but for him, the child would have perished in the waters of the river.

Well treated and well cared for, Llanga had then been carried into the Waggdian village. Li-Maï had not been long in regaining his strength, for he was suffering only from starvation and weariness. After having been Llanga's *protégé*, he had become his protector, and his father and mother had shown themselves very grateful towards the young native. Is not gratitude found among animals for the services rendered them? and so why should it not exist among beings who are superior to them? . . . In short, that very morning Llanga had been brought by Li-Maï before this hut. What for? He had not known. But he had heard voices and when he had listened to them he had recognised those of John Cort and Max Huber . . .

That was what had happened since they had been separated on the dam of the Rio Johausen.

"Good, Llanga, good!" said Max Huber, "but we're dying of hunger and before going on with your story, if you can, by grace of your protectors . . ."

Llanga went out and was not slow in returning with some food, a large piece of grilled buffalo, nicely salted, half a dozen fruits including some fresh bananas, and in a calabash some clear water sweetened with fruit juice.

It will be realised that conversation then ceased. The

three men were in too great need of food to show themselves fussy about its quality ... Of the piece of buffalo meat, the bread, and the bananas they left nothing but the bones and the skins.

Then John Cort asked the young native if there were many of the Waggdis.

"Many ... many! ... I've seen a lot of them ... in the streets and in the huts," Llanga told him.

"As many as those in those villages we passed through?"

"Yes."

"And they never go down?"

"Yes ... yes ... to hunt ... to get roots and fruit ... to draw water ..."

"And they talk?"

"Yes, but I can't understand them ... and yet ... a few words sometimes ... some words ... that I know ... like Li-Maï."

"And his father and mother?"

"Oh, they've been very good to me ... what I brought you came from them ..."

"I'm longing to tell them how grateful I am," Max Huber declared.

"And this village in the treetops, what's it called?"

"Ngala."

"And has this village a chief?"

"Yes."

"You've seen him?"

"No, but I've heard that he's called Msélo-Tala-Tala."

"Native words!" exclaimed Khamis.

"What do they mean?"

"Father Looking-glass," the foreloper replied.

And indeed it is thus that the Congolese speak of a man who wears spectacles.

CHAPTER XIV

THE WAGGDIS

HIS MAJESTY Msélo-Tala-Tala, king of this people of the Waggdis, ruler of this village in the treetops, was not this real enough to realise the *desiderata* of Max Huber? In his fertile French imagination had he not foreseen, in the depths of this mysterious Oubanghi Forest, new peoples, unknown cities, a whole world of extraordinary creatures whose existence had never been suspected? . . . He had got his wish, and he was the first to applaud himself for having so much foresight. Nor did he stop until John very reasonably commented:

"That's understood, my dear friend. Like all poets you are something of a prophet, and you prophesied . . ."

"Quite right, my dear John, but whatever this semi-human tribe of the Waggdis may be, I don't mean to end my life in their capital . . ."

"Well, my dear Max, we've got to stay here long enough to study this race from the ethnological and anthropological point of view, so that we can publish a great volume which will revolutionise the Learned Societies of both worlds . . ."

"Right," replied Max Huber, "we'll make our observations, we'll compare notes, we'll compile these regarding the whole question of anthropormorphy, but on two conditions . . ."

"And what's the first?"

"That they let us go free—I'm depending on it—to come and go in this village . . ."

"And the second?"

JULES VERNE

"That after letting us roam about freely, we'll be able to get away whenever it suits us . . ."

Might not Max Huber have spoken too decidedly in counting on their being allowed to roam freely about the village? And when it came to leaving it at their convenience? . . . And if neither he nor his companions should ever reappear at the factory, who would think of looking for them in this village of Ngala in the depths of the great Forest? . . . When nobody returned from the caravan, who would doubt that it had completely perished somewhere in the Upper Oubanghi? . . .

As for the question of knowing whether the three men were or were not prisoners in the hut, that was quickly settled. The door turned upon its liana fastenings and Li-Maï appeared.

The little thing first went straight up to Llanga and lavished upon him a thousand caresses, which were very heartily returned. John Cort took this opportunity of examining this strange creature more carefully. But as the door was open Max Huber suggested that they should go out and mingle with this treetop population.

So there they were outside, guided by the little savage—for might he not be called that?—who was holding hands with his friend Llanga. They found themselves in the centre of a sort of square, across which the Waggdis were "going about their business."

The square was planted with trees, or rather it was sheltered by the tops of the trees whose massive trunks supported this aerial construction. Built a hundred feet above the ground on the strongest of their branches, and formed of cross-pieces firmly fixed together by wedges and lianas, a bed of beaten earth had been spread out upon its surface, and as the points of support were as secure as they were numerous, this artificial ground did not quiver beneath their feet.

While the strangers were walking about, the Waggdis, men, women and children, looked at them without showing any surprise. They were exchanging a few remarks in a raucous voice, brief phrases spoken hurriedly and unintelligible words. Every now and again the foreloper thought he could hear several expressions in the Congolese language; nor was this surprising for Li-Maï had several times used the word "*Ngora.*" This seemed inexplicable. But what was even more so, was that John Cort was struck by the repetition of two or three German words, among others that of *Vater* ("Father"), and he made this peculiarity known to his comrades.

"What do you expect, my dear John?" Max Huber replied. "I expect everything, even that these fellows should prod me in the stomach and say, 'Well, old man, how's it going?'"

From time to time Li-Maï, letting go Llanga's hand, went from one to the other of the natives, a lively joyous child. He seemed proud to be leading the strangers along the village streets. It was clear that he was not taking them at random, that he was leading them somewhere, and all they had to do was to follow their five-year-old guide.

These primitives, as John Cort called them, were not completely naked. Without speaking of the russet fur which partly covered their bodies, men and women were draped in a sort of waist-cloth of vegetable tissue, somewhat similar to, though more crudely manufactured than, those women in other parts of Africa.

What John Cort specially pointed out was that the Waggdian heads, rounded and reduced to the dimensions of the microcephalic, and with almost a human facial angle, showed little prognathism. Moreover, the eyebrows did not beetle as do those of most of the simian race. Their hair was the fleecy wool of the natives of equatorial Africa, with the beard little developed.

"And no prehensile foot . . ." John Cort declared.

"And no caudal appendage," Max Huber added, "not even the smallest stump of a tail!"

"Quite true," John Cort replied, "and that's in itself a sign of superiority. The anthropoid apes have no tails, no pouched cheeks, no callosities. They can go on foot or on all fours as they prefer. But it has been pointed out that the apes who walk upright don't use the soles of their feet; they support themselves on the backs of their bent toes. Well, it isn't so with the Waggdis, and their stride is absolutely like that of man, we've got to admit that."

This comment was quite accurate and it was no doubt a question of a new race. On the other hand, as regards the foot, certain anthropologists declare that there is no difference between that of the monkey and that of man, and that the latter would even have an opposable great-toe had his foot not been deformed by the use of boots.

There were moreover, physical similarities between the two races. The apes who walk upright are the least petulant and make the fewest grimaces, in short they are the gravest and most serious of the species. And it was just this character of seriousness which was displayed in the attitude as well as in the acts of these inhabitants of Ngala. What was more, when John Cort examined them attentively, he was able to realise that their system of dentation was identical with that of man.

These resemblances could then, up to a certain point, support the doctrine of the variability of species, the upwards evolution postulated by Darwin. This has even been regarded as decisive by comparison between specimens of the highest of the monkeys and the most primitive of humanity. Linnaeus has put forward the opinion that there have been men who were troglodytes (cave dwellers), an expression which anyhow could not be applied to the Waggdis, who live in the treetops.

Vogt has even claimed that man has descended from three great types of apes. The Orang, a brachycephalic type with long brown hair, would, according to him, be the ancestor of the Negritos. The Chimpanzee, a dolichocephalic type, with less massive jaws, would be the

THE VILLAGE IN THE TREETOPS

ancestor of the Negroes. Finally from the Gorilla, specialised by the development of the chest, the form of the foot, the gait, and the osteological character of body and limbs, had descended the White Men.

That these similarities may however be opposed by differences of the first importance in the intellectual and moral order—differences which the Darwinian theory ought to take into consideration.

It is necessary then, while taking into account the distinctive characters of three types of apes, without however admitting that their brain contains the twelve million cells and the four million fibres of the human brain, to believe that they belong to a superior race of the animal kingdom. But it must not be inferred that man is a perfected ape or the ape a degenerate man.

As to the microcephalic types, which it is claimed are intermediate between man and the ape, a species vainly predicted by the anthropologists and vainly sought for, that missing link which should attach the animal kingdom to that of man, could it be admitted that it was represented by these Waggdis? . . . Had the strange chances of their voyage reserved its discovery for this Frenchman and this American? . . . Yet even if this unknown people had a physical resemblance to the human race it would still be necessary for the Waggdis to have the moral and religious characters peculiar to man, not to mention the faculty of conceiving abstraction and generalisations, an aptitude for the arts, science, and letters. Then only would it be possible to decide once and for all between the theories of the monogenists and the polygenists.

But one thing certain in short, was, that the Waggdians spoke. Not limited only to instincts, they had ideas—the use of speech presupposed this—and words which could be joined together to form a language. More than cries eked out by glance and gesture, they used an articulate speech, having for its basis a series of sounds and con-

JULES VERNE

ventional expressions which had been bequeathed to them by atavism.

This was what had most struck John Cort. This faculty, which implies the participation of memory, indicated an inborn racial influence.

Meanwhile, while studying the customs and habits of this woodland tribe, the three men were making their way through the village streets.

Was it large, the village? ... Its circumference could not be less than two miles, "and," as Max Huber put it, "though it's only a nest, at any rate, it's a big nest!"

Most of the huts, fresh with foliage and built like hives, stood wide open. The women were busily devoting themselves to their somewhat rudimentary household duties. The children were numerous, the youngest being suckled by their mothers. Some of the men were gathering fruits among the branches, others were going down the ladder to devote themselves to their usual occupations. Some returned with pieces of game, others brought back jars which they had filled with water from the stream.

"It's a pity," said Max Huber, "that we don't know their language!"

But as the Waggdian language, according to what they had heard from Li-Maï contained some native words, Khamis tried a few of the most usual when he spoke to the child.

But Li-Maï did not seem to understand. And yet in front of the two friends he had used the word "*Ngora*" when he was lying on the raft. Since then Llanga declared that he had learned from the boy's father that the village was called "Ngala" and the chief of the village "Msélo-Tala-Tala."

At last, after an hour's walk, the three men reached the end of the village. There rose a more important hut. Built between the branches of an enormous tree, its front wall lined with reeds, its roof lost itself in the foliage.

THE VILLAGE IN THE TREETOPS

Was this hut the palace of the king, the sanctuary of the witch-doctors, the temple of the spirits, like those of most of the savage tribes in Africa, Australia and the Pacific Islands? . . . The opportunity had come to get some more definite information from Li-Maï. So John Cort, taking him by the shoulders and turning him towards the hut, asked "Msélo-Tala-Tala?"

A movement of the head was the only reply he received. There dwelt the Chief of Ngala village, his Waggdian Majesty.

And, without further ceremony, Max Huber walked deliberately towards the hut. This brought a change of attitude from the child, who held him back and showed a real fear. Max Huber persisted, several times repeating "Msélo-Tala-Tala?"

But just as he was going to reach the hut, the child ran up to him and stopped him from going further.

So it was forbidden to approach the royal house? . . . And indeed two sentinels had just got up and, brandishing their weapons, a sort of iron-wood axe and an assegai, they prevented him from going in.

A few minutes later the visitors arrived in a more sheltered part of the village, where the foliage of the treetops was closely knit together.

Li-Maï stopped before a large hut whose roof was made of large leaves of the banana-tree, woven together like those which the foreloper had used to build a shelter on the raft. A sort of beaten earth formed the threshold of this hut, reached by a door which then stood open. The child pointed it out to Llanga, who recognised it at once. "That's it," he said.

Inside, one large room. In its depths a bed of dry grass, which could easily be renewed. In the corner several stones forming a hearth, on which pieces of wood were glowing. For the only utensils, two or three calabashes—an earthenware jar filled with water and two pots made of the same material. These woodland creatures did not use forks, they ate with their fingers. Here

JULES VERNE

and there, on a shelf fixed to the wall, fruits, roots, a little cooked meat, half-a-dozen birds plucked ready for the next meal; and hanging on large thorns, some strips of bark-cloth.

A Waggdian man and a Waggdian woman got up when Khamis and his companions entered the hut. "*Ngora!* . . . *Ngora!* . . . *Lo-Maï* . . . *Lo-Maï* . . ." said the child.

And the former added as if he thought he would be better understood, "*Vater . . . Vater! . . .*"

This German word for "father" he pronounced very badly. But what could be more extraordinary than that a word of this language should be in the mouth of these creatures? . . .

Scarcely had he entered when Llanga went straight to the mother. She opened her arms to him and pressed him against her, caressing him with her hands and showing her gratitude for him who had rescued her child.

John Cort noticed that the father was tall and well-proportioned; he looked strong; his arms were a little longer than those of man, his hands large and firm, his legs slightly bowed, the soles of his feet firmly planted on the ground.

He had the almost clear complexion of those native tribes which are more carnivorous than vegetarian, a short fleecy beard, black woolly hair. A sort of fleece covered his whole body. His head was of medium size, his jaws but slightly projecting; his eyes, with their glowing pupils, shone brightly.

Just as gracious was the mother, with a sweet pleasant appearance, a glance which devoted great affection, excellent teeth of remarkable whiteness, and—among what individuals of the weaker sex does not coquetry show itself?—some flowers in her hair as well as—an inexplicable detail—some pieces of glass and some ivory pearls. This young Waggdian woman resembled the Kaffirs of the South, with her arms round and well shaped, her delicate wrists, her plump hands and her feet which

THE VILLAGE IN THE TREETOPS

would have made more than one European lady feel envious. Over her woolly fleece had been thrown some bark-cloth, fastened with a belt. At her neck hung one of Dr. Johausen's medals, similar to that which the child was wearing.

To the great regret of John Cort it was impossible to converse with Lo-Maï and La-Maï. But it was clear that these two primitives were anxious to fulfill all the duties of Waggdian hospitality. The father offered some fruits, and the guests accepted these and ate several, to the extreme satisfaction of the family.

In the conversation of these Waggdis the questions and answers were short, merely consisting of two or three words, all of which began with the letters, *Ng, Mgou, Ms,* as among the people of the Congo. The mother seemed less talkative than the father and perhaps her tongue lacked the power possessed by the feminine tongues of the two worlds, that of wagging a dozen thousand times a minute. John Cort was most surprised to realise that these primitives were using certain Congolese and German words, much disfigured in the pronunciation.

After a quarter of an hour spent within the hut the three men left it, led by Lo-Maï and his child. They went back to the hut to which they had been led and which they were to occupy until ... Always that question, and perhaps it would not be left to themselves to answer it.

There they made their farewells. Lo-Maï gave a last kiss to the young native. Then he held out not his paw like a dog nor his hand like an ape, but both hands. John Cort and Max Huber shook them more cordially than did Khamis.

CHAPTER XV

THREE WEEKS' STUDY

AND NOW, how long were the three men and Llanga to stay in the village? . . . Would anything happen to change the position, which never ceased to be disquieting? . . . They felt they were always being watched, that they could never get away. And anyhow, even if they succeeded in escaping, how, in the midst of this impenetrable region of the great forest, could they reach its edge, how could they find the course of the Rio Johausen? . . .

After having so much wanted something extraordinary, Max Huber realised that the longer the situation lasted the more it lost its charm. So he showed himself the most impatient, the most anxious to return to the Oubanghi Basin, and to reach the factory at Libreville, where he and John Cort would not lack for a welcome.

For his part the foreloper was furious at this stroke of bad luck which had made him fall into the paws—in his opinion they were paws—of these inferior creatures. He did not seek to conceal the complete distrust which they inspired in him, for to him they did not seem to differ greatly from the tribes of Central Africa. Khamis felt a sort of jealousy, and although this was instinctive and unconscious, the two friends realised it quite well. Indeed he was no less anxious than Max Huber to leave Ngala, and everything that seemed likely to make it possible he would do.

It was John Cort who felt the least need for haste. To study these primitives had a special interest for him. To

THE VILLAGE IN THE TREETOPS

learn their customs, their existence in all its details, their ethnological character, their moral value, to know how far they went towards the condition of the animals, a few weeks would have sufficed.

But could they be sure that their stay among the Waggdis would not last longer than that . . . months, perhaps even years? . . . And what would be the outcome of this astonishing adventure?

At any rate the three men did not seem to be threatened with ill-treatment. There was no doubt that these woodland creatures recognised their intellectual superiority. But it was still extraordinary that they had shown no surprise at seeing these representatives of the human race. Anyhow, if the latter were to try to use force to get away, they would expose themselves to violence which it would be better to avoid.

"What we've got to do," said Max Huber, "is to get into communication with Father Looking-Glass, the bespectacled sovereign, and persuade him to set us free."

Indeed it ought not to be impossible to have an interview with His Majesty Msélo-Tala-Tala—unless strangers were forbidden to contemplate his august person. But if they got into his presence, how should they exchange questions and answers? . . . Even in the Congolese language they would not understand one another! . . . And what would be the outcome? . . . Would not it be to the interest of the Waggdis, by keeping these strangers with them, to assure the secret of this existence of an unknown race in the depths of the Oubanghian Forest?

And yet, according to John Cort, this imprisonment in the treetop village had extenuating circumstances; the science of comparative anthropology would profit by it, the world of knowledge would be stirred by this discovery of a new race. As to the way in which it would end . . . "Devil take it if I know," Max Huber repeated; he was neither a Garner nor a Johausen.

When the three, followed by Llanga, had gone back

JULES VERNE

into their hut, they noticed several changes which they did not find displeasing. First, one of the Waggdis was busy "doing out the room," if one can use this somewhat colloquial expression. And indeed John Cort had already noticed that these primitives had instincts of cleanliness which most of the animals lack.

Moreover, several objects had been placed on the floor—for the furniture included neither table nor chairs —a few uncouth utensils, pots and jars of Waggdian manufacture. Here fruit of several varieties, there some meat freshly cooked. Raw flesh suits only carnivorous animals, and it is rare to find in the lowest degree of the human scale beings of which it forms the sole food.

"And whoever can make fire," John Cort declared, "uses it to prepare their food. So I'm not a bit surprised that the Waggdis live on cooked meat."

The hut also possessed a hearth, formed of a flat stone, the smoke being lost through the branches of the tree which supported it.

As soon as the four opened the door, the Waggdis stopped work.

He was a youth about twenty years old, agile and with an intelligent face, and he pointed to the objects which had been brought in. Among them the three men, not without an extreme satisfaction, saw their carbines. These were a little rusty but it would be easy to get them into condition.

"Well," exclaimed Max Huber, "they're welcome . . . and if we have to . . ."

"We'd make use of them," added John Cort, "if only we had our box of cartridges . . ."

"There it is," and the foreloper pointed to the metal box, placed on the left close by the door. This box and these weapons, it will be recalled, he had had the presence of mind to throw on the rocks of the dam just as the raft crashed against it. It was there that the Waggdis had found them and taken them to Ngala village.

"As they've given us our carbines," commented Max Huber, "do they realise what firearms are for?"

"I don't know," John Cort replied, "but what they do know is that they mustn't keep what doesn't belong to them, and that's an argument in favour of their morality."

All the same the question Max Huber had asked did not fail to be important.

"Kollo . . . Kollo! . . ."

This word, clearly pronounced, was spoken several times and in pronouncing it the young Waggdi lifted his hand to his forehead; then, he touched his chest, as though to say; "Kollo . . . that's me!"

John Cort assumed that this must be the name of their new servant, and when he had repeated it half-a-dozen times, Kollo testified his delight by a prolonged laugh. For they laughed, these primitives, and this had to be borne in mind from the anthropological point of view.

These Waggdis anyhow seemed mild by nature, little quarrelsome and—it must be stressed—less curious and less surprised by the presence of these strangers than would have been the most backward of African or Australian savages. The sight of two white men and two Congolese natives did not astonish them as it would have astonished a native of Africa. It left them indifferent and they did not show themselves indiscreet: there were no signs of inquisitiveness or snobbery.

Yet in acrobatics, in climbing among the trees, in leaping from branch to branch, in swarming up and down the staircase, they would have broken all records of circus gymnastics.

While displaying their physical qualities the Waggdis also gave proofs of an extraordinary accuracy of eye. When they went hunting birds they brought them down with small arrows, and similar skill would not have been lacking when they hunted game through the adjoining forest. It was then that Max Huber would have wanted to go with them, as much to admire their prowess as hunters as to try to give them the slip.

Yes, to escape—that was what the prisoners were always dreaming about. But flight was practicable only by the one stairway, and on its upper landing were a squad of warriors whose watchfulness it would have been difficult to elude.

Several times Max Huber had wanted to shoot the birds which abounded in the trees, and which the Waggdis ate so freely. But he and his companions were every day supplied with game, very plentiful in the Oubanghi forest. Their servant Kollo did not let them lack for anything; every day he renewed the supply of fresh water for the needs of the household and the supply of fuel to keep up the fire. Moreover, it would have been unwise to reveal the power of their weapons. Much better to keep it secret and then, if necessary, to use them in offence or defence.

If their guests were supplied with meat, it was because the Waggdis fed on it themselves, sometimes grilled on the embers, sometimes boiled in the earthern vessels which they had made. This was what Kollo did for their benefit, accepting the help of Llanga, failing that of Khamis who had refused it in his native pride.

One question which interested John Cort was that of fire. How did these primitives make it? . . . Was it by rubbing a piece of hardwood on a piece of softwood after the style of the savages? . . . No, they did not use that method; they used flints, getting sparks by striking them together. These sparks were enough to kindle the hair of a certain fruit which possessed all the properties of tinder.

A stream of water, full of fish, which passed under Ngala, contained the same species as those found by Khamis and his companions in the Rio Johausen. But was it navigable, and did the Waggdis use boats? . . . That was important to know if the prisoners wanted to get away.

THE VILLAGE IN THE TREETOPS

This watercourse was visible from the end of the village furthest from the royal hut. But standing near the last of the trees they could see its bed, thirty to forty feet wide. Beyond, it lost itself between the magnificent trees.

Yes, the Waggdis certainly knew how to build boats—an art not unknown even among the most backward people of Oceania. They were more than rafts but less than canoes, mere trunks of trees hollowed out with fire and axe. They were propelled with paddles, and, when the wind favored them, with sails spread on two spars; the sails were made of a bark rendered supple by being well beaten with mallets of extremely hard ironwood.

What John Cort realised, however, was that these primitives did not use either vegetables or cereals in their food. They did not know how to cultivate sorgum, or millet, or rice, or manioc—ordinary work among the peoples of Central Africa.

Having made these observations, he was anxious to know whether the Waggdis had any feelings of morality or religion.

One day Max Huber asked him the result of his researches into this subject.

"They have a certain morality, a certain probity," he replied, "they can distinguish between right and wrong; they also have the idea of property. In my opinion the Waggdis understand the difference between yours and mine. I noticed this when one of them had stolen some fruit from a hut into which he had crawled.

"I should add that these primitives are distinguished by an institution which makes them akin to humanity..."

"What is that?"

"The family, regularly formed among them, the life in common of the father and mother, the care they lavish upon the children, the continuation of paternal and filial affection. Haven't we noticed it with Lo-Maï?..."

"The Waggdis also have purely human feelings. Look at our Kollo, doesn't he blush under the action of some moral influence? . . . Whether that's due to shame, timidity, modesty or confusion, the four feelings which bring a blush to the human forehead, it is undeniable that that effect is produced in him. So he has feelings . . . so he has a soul!"

"Then," asked Max Huber, "as these Waggdis possess so many human qualities, why not admit them into the ranks of humanity?"

"Because they seem to lack an idea which is common to all men, my dear Max."

"And by that you mean?"

"The conception of a Supreme Being. In one word, religion, which is found among the most savage tribes. I cannot see that they adore any divinities . . . neither idols nor priests . . ."

"Unless," replied Max Huber, "their divinity may not be this very king, Msélo-Tala-Tala, of whom they won't let us see even the tip of his nose!"

Several times the foreloper attempted to leave the village, but he was always unsuccessful: the warriors who guarded the ladder intervened, not without a certain violence. Once, especially, Khamis would have been maltreated if Lo-Maï, who had been attracted to the scene, had not come to his rescue.

There was then a heated discussion between the latter and a great burly fellow who was called Raggi. From the garment of skin that he wore, from the weapons which hung at his belt, from the feathers which ornamented his head, there was reason to think that he was the chief of the warriors. If only by his ferocious appearance, his imperious gestures, and his natural brutality, he seemed to be made for command.

Following these attempts, the two friends had hoped that they would be sent before His Majesty and that they would at last see this king whom his subjects concealed with jealous care in the depths of the royal dwelling . . . Their hopes came to nothing. It was probable that Raggi had complete authority, and there was

THE VILLAGE IN THE TREETOPS

no point in exposing themselves to his anger by making another attempt. Thus the chances of escape were very small unless the Waggdis, were they to attack some neighbouring village, should be attacked in their turn.

If an attack should take place, it might perhaps give them a chance of leaving Ngala . . . But what would happen then?

What was more, the village was never threatened during these first weeks except by certain animals, which Khamis and his companions had not yet met with in the great forest. If the Waggdis spent their lives in Ngala, if they returned at nightfall, they nevertheless had built certain huts on the banks of the rio. It might have been called a little river harbour in which were drawn up their fishing-boats, which they had to protect against the hippopotami and crocodiles so numerous in the African waters.

One day, on 9th April, a violent tumult broke out. Cries resounded from the direction of the river. Was it an attack launched against the Waggdis by beings similar to themselves? . . . Thanks to its situation, no doubt, the village was safe from invasion. But if fire were put to the trees which supported it, its destruction would have taken only a few hours. And the methods which these primitive beings might have employed against their neighbours, it was not impossible that the latter would try to use against them.

As soon as the uproar boke out, Raggi and about thirty of the warriors, making for the ladder, descended with the agility of monkeys. Meanwhile the two white men, and the foreloper, guided by Lo-Maï reached the side of the village from which they could see the watercourse.

It was an invasion directed against the huts built on the river bank. A horde, not of natives, but of creatures resembling hippopotami, had come dashing out of the undergrowth and were smashing everything in their way.

Between the branches of the trees John Cort and his

friends could watch the struggle. It was short and not without danger, and the warriors displayed the greatest courage. Using hunting-spears and axes in preference to bows and assegais, they rushed forward with an ardour which equalled the fury of the assailants. They attacked them face to face, dealing blows on their head with their axes, piercing their flanks with their spears. In short, after an hour of fighting, the animals were making off and streams of blood were mingling with the waters of the river.

Max Huber had thought of taking part in the fight. To fetch his carbine and that of John Cort, to open fire from the village upon the horde, to bring down the animals with a hail of bullets, to the extreme surprise of the Waggdis, would neither have taken long nor been difficult. But the more thoughtful John Cort, supported by the foreloper, pacified his friend.

"No," he told him, "we must reserve our intervention for more decisive circumstances . . . when you can use the lightning, my dear Max . . ."

"You're quite right, John, you must keep it for the proper time . . . and as it's not yet time to thunder we'll put our thunder away!"

CHAPTER XVI

HIS MAJESTY MSÉLO-TALA-TALA

THAT DAY, or rather that afternoon of 15th April, a change took place in the calm habits of the Waggdians. For three weeks the prisoners in Ngala had found no opportunity of resuming their journey towards the Oubanghi. Closely watched, confined within the impassable limits of the village, they could not get away.

THE VILLAGE IN THE TREETOPS

Certainly it was quite open to them—and more particularly to John Cort—to study the manners of these types midway between the most perfect of the anthropoids and man, to see what instincts united them with the animal kingdom, what tincture of reasoning power brought them towards the human race. Here was a real treasury of comments to employ in discussions of the Darwinian Theory. But to make this available to the world of knowledge, they would have to find their way back to the French Congo and return to Libreville . . .

The weather was perfect. A brilliant sun flooded with heat and light the foliage which sheltered the village in the treetops. Though it had passed the zenith three hours before, the slope of its rays did not modify its heat.

The contacts of John Cort and Max Huber with the Maï family had been frequent. Not a day elapsed without that family coming into their hut or without them going into theirs. It was a real exchange of visits—all that was lacking were the visiting cards! The child hardly ever left Llanga and felt a real affection for the young native.

Unfortunately, it was still impossible to comprehend the language of these primitives; this was reduced to a few words which sufficed for the paucity of their ideas. Though John Cort had been able to gather the significance of several terms, that did not allow him to converse with the inhabitants of Ngala. He was still surprised to find that several native expressions figured in the Waggdian vocabulary—perhaps a dozen. Did not this indicate that the Waggdis had been in contact with the tribes of the Oubanghi—if only with some Congolese native who had never got back to the Congo? . . . A fairly plausible hypothesis, it will be agreed. What was more, an occasional word of German origin escaped from the lips of Lo-Maï, but always pronounced so incorrectly that it could scarcely be recognised.

This was something which John Cort regarded as absolutely inexplicable. Even if it were supposed that the natives and the Waggdis had met, was it admissible that the latter had been in contact with the Germans of the Cameroons? . . . If so, neither the American nor the Frenchman had heard any tidings of that discovery. Although John Cort could speak German fairly fluently he had never had the opportunity of using it, because Lo-Maï only knew two or three of its words.

Among other phrases borrowed from the natives, that of Msélo-Tala-Tala, which was applied to the ruler of this tribe, was the most often used. It has already been explained what a desire the two friends felt to be received by this invisible potentate. Certainly, every time that he pronounced that name, Lo-Maï bowed his head in token of deep respect. But when their walks took them near the royal hut, if they showed the slightest signs of getting into it, he stopped them, pushed them aside, dragged them to right or left. His manner made them realise that nobody had the right to cross the threshold of the sacred dwelling.

Now it happened that this afternoon, a little before three, the Lo-Maï family came to find Khamis and his companions.

It was at once obvious that the family was wearing its finest clothing; the father with a magnificent feathered head-gear and draped in his bark mantle; the mother wearing a petticoat of native make, a few green leaves in her hair, and a necklace of glass and tiny pieces of metal, the child a small loin-cloth girded about his waist—"their Sunday best," as Max Huber put it.

And on seeing this formal attire, "What does this mean? . . ." he asked. "Are they thinking of paying us a special visit? . . ."

"It must be a festival," John Cort replied, "is it a question of paying homage to some god? . . . That would be an interesting point, for it would settle the question of their religion . . ."

THE VILLAGE IN THE TREETOPS

Before he could finish his phrase, Lo-Maï said as though in answer, "Msélo-Tala-Tala..."

"The Father with spectacles!" Max translated, and he went out of the hut with the idea that His Majesty was passing at that very moment.

He was soon disillusioned! He could not see even His Majesty's shadow!

Yet it was clear that all Ngala was in movement. From everywhere was coming a crowd as joyful and as sumptuously clad as the Maï family. A great assembly of the people, some walking in procession along the streets towards the western end of the village and holding each other's hands like peasants out on a spree, others gambolling from tree to tree like monkeys.

"There's something fresh happening..." declared John Cort, stopping on the threshold of his hut.

"We'll go and see," Max Huber replied. Then turning to Lo-Maï, "Msélo-Tala-Tala?..." he repeated.

"Msélo-Tala-Tala!" replied Lo-Maï crossing his arms and bowing his head.

John Cort and Max Huber came to the conclusion that the Waggdian population was going to greet this bespectacled king, who would soon appear in all his glory.

They themselves had no ceremonial costume to wear. They were reduced to their only hunting outfit, much used and rather dirty, and to their linen, which they kept as clean as they could. So they had no toilet to make in honour of His Majesty, and when the Maï family came out of the hut they followed with Llanga. Khamis, who did not care to mix with his inferiors, "kept himself to himself," and got busy arranging the utensils in preparation for a meal and in cleaning the firearms. Was it not essential to be ready for any eventuality, and might not the hour be coming when he would have to make use of them?

So John Cort and Max Huber let themselves be guided by Lo-Maï across this village, which now seemed so lively. There were no streets in the strict sense of the word. Scattered at the whim of their owners, the huts conformed to the growth of the trees, or rather to that of the treetops which sheltered them.

The people were hurrying together. At least a thousand of the Waggdis were making for the part of Ngala at whose end rose the Royal Hut.

"It would be impossible to be more like a human crowd!" John Cort pointed out, "the same movements, the same ways of showing their satisfaction by cries and gestures . . ."

"And by making faces," added Max Huber, "and this is what connects these strange creatures with the apes!"

And, indeed, the Waggdis, usually so serious and reserved and uncommunicative, had never shown themselves so expansive, or made so many gestures. And there was still that inexplicable indifference towards the strangers, to whom they did not seem to pay any attention—an attention which would have obsessed any African tribe.

This was not exactly "human!"

After a long walk, Max Huber and John Cort arrived at the main square, which was sheltered by the tops of the last trees on the forest side, whose fertile branches surrounded the royal palace. In front were arrayed the warriors complete with all their weapons; they were clad in antelope skins attached by fine lianas, and their heads were covered with horns, which made them look like a herd of cattle. As for "Colonel" Raggi, helmeted in a buffalo's head, a bow over his shoulder, an axe in his waist-belt, a hunting-spear in his hand, he was parading in front of the Waggdian army.

"It looks," John Cort suggested, "as if the king is getting ready to review his troops . . ."

"And if he doesn't come," replied Max Huber, "it must be because he never shows himself to his faithful subjects! . . . It's not to be supposed that invisibility adds prestige to a monarch and so perhaps he . . ."

Addressing himself to Lo-Maï and eking out his words

THE VILLAGE IN THE TREETOPS

by a gesture, he asked, "Msélo-Tala-Tala's coming out?"

An affirmative sign from Lo-Maï, who seemed to be saying, "Later . . . later . . ."

"That doesn't matter," Max Huber replied, "so long as we are allowed to contemplate his august countenance . . ."

"Well, while we're waiting," John Cort replied, "don't let's lose anything of this spectacle."

But what seemed queerest was that the center of the square, in which there were no trees, was left vacant. The crowd thronged round it with the aim, no doubt, of taking part in the festival whenever the King should appear on the threshold of his palace. Would they prostrate themselves before him? . . . Would they overwhelm him with adoration? . . .

"After all," John Cort pointed out, "we needn't consider such adoration from the religious point of view, because it would only be addressed to a man . . ."

"At least," Max Huber replied, "so long as this man isn't made of wood or stone . . . so long as this potentate isn't an idol of the sort worshipped by the natives of Polynesia . . ."

"If so, my dear Max, nothing will be lacking to the Ngala people to be complete human beings . . . They'll have the right to be classified as men, just like the natives you were talking about . . ."

"Assuming that the latter deserve it!" replied Max Huber, in tones that were little flattering to the Polynesian race.

"Certainly, my dear Max, because they believe in the existence of some deity of other . . . Never has anybody taken into his head to class them among the animals, even among those which occupy the highest rank in the animal kingdom!"

Thanks to the family of Lo-Maï, the two men and Llanga were able to place themselves where they could see everything.

As the crowd had left the centre of the square open,

the young people of both sexes were able to dance, while their elders began to drink like the heroes of a Dutch festival.

What these woodland creatures were swallowing was some fermented drink flavoured with tamarisk bark. And it must have been extremely alcoholic, for heads were not slow in getting heated and legs to stagger disquietingly.

It is difficult to say whether there were more grimaces than contortions and even somersaults. To sum it up, in these choreographic attitudes there were to be seen less of the man than of the monkey. And, indeed, not the monkey educated for exhibitions at a show, no! . . . but the monkey left to its natural instincts. Moreover the dances were not executed only to the sound of a general tumult. It was to the tune of the most rudimentary instruments, calabashes covered with a skin and struck with vigorous blows, and hollow stems shaped into whistles, into which a dozen strong executants were blowing as if to burst their lungs. No! . . . never had a more deafening hullabaloo distressed white ears!

"They don't seem to have any idea of keeping time," commented John Cort.

"No more than they do of keeping tune," replied Max Huber.

"On the whole, they're sensitive to music, my dear Max . . ."

"And the animals are too, my dear John—some of them, at any rate. To my mind, music is an inferior art addressed to an inferior sense. On the other hand, when it comes to painting, to sculpture, to literature, never has any animal felt their charm, and never have you seen even the most intelligent show themselves moved by a picture or the recital of a poetic effusion!"

However this might be, the Waggdis resembled man not only because they felt the effects of music, but because they themselves put this art into practice.

Two hours passed thus, to the extreme impatience

THE VILLAGE IN THE TREETOPS

of Max Huber. What annoyed him most was that Msélo-Tala-Tala did not deign to put himself out to receive the homage of his subjects.

But the festival was going on with redoubled cries and dances. The drinks were stimulating the violence of drunkenness, and it might well be wondered what scenes of disorder were threatening to follow when, suddenly, the tumult ended. Everybody calmed down, crouched on his haunches, and remained motionless. A complete silence followed those noisy demonstrations, the deafening uproar of the tom-toms, the shrill whistle of the flutes.

At that moment the door of the royal dwelling opened and the warriors formed a hedge on either side.

"At last!" exclaimed Max Huber, "at last we're going to see him, this king of the woods."

But it was not His Majesty who emerged from the hut. Some sort of article, covered with a cloth made of leaves, was brought into the middle of the square. And what was the very natural surprise of the two friends when they recognised in that article a common barrel-organ! . . . Most probably this sacred instrument figured only in the great ceremonies of Ngala and no doubt its auditors listened to airs more or less varied with their hearts ravished like dilettentes!

"But it's Dr. Johausen's organ!" said John Cort.

"It can only be that antediluvian contraption," Max Huber replied, "and now at last I can understand how it was, on the night when we came beneath the village in Ngala, I had the vague impression of hearing that pitiless waltz from the *Freyschütz* above my head!"

"And you never said anything about it, Max?"

"I thought I must have been dreaming, John."

"As for that organ," John Cort added, "it must certainly have been the Waggdis who brought it from the Doctor's hut."

"And after having done some harm to that poor man!" Max Huber added.

A superb Waggdi—plainly the leader of the local orchestra—came and placed himself before the instrument and began to turn the handle. At once, to the very real pleasure of the audience, the waltz in question, with several of its notes lacking, began to unroll. It was a concert which followed the choreographic exercises. The crowd listened while nodding their heads—out of time, it is true. Certainly they didn't seem to feel that impulse to go round in circles which a waltz imparts to the civilised people of both worlds.

And gravely, as though impressed with the importance of his task, the Waggdi went on working his musical box. But did they know in Ngala that the barrel-organ contained other tunes? . . . That was what John Cort wondered. Certainly these primitives could never have discovered by chance the procedure by which, on pressing a button, they could replace Weber's melody by another.

What happened, however, was that after half an hour devoted to the waltz from the *Freyschütz,* here was the executant pressing a button on the side, just as a street player would have done to the instrument suspended from his shoulder-strap.

"Well, my word . . . that's too much, that is!" exclaimed Max Huber. Too much indeed, unless someone had taught these woodland creatures the secret of the mechanism and how they could extract from this barbaric affair all the melodies it held in its heart! . . . The handle was again put into movement and then a German air was followed by a French air, one of the most popular, the plaintive song from the *Grâce de Dieu.*

Everybody knows this "masterpiece" of Loïsa Puget. There is nobody who does not know that the tune goes on in *La* minor for sixteen bars and that the chorus goes on in *La* major, following all the traditions of contemporary art.

"Oh, the unhappy creature! . . . oh, the miserable wretch! . . ." howled Max Huber, whose exclamations

THE VILLAGE IN THE TREETOPS

aroused very significant murmurs among the audience.

"What wretch?" John Cort asked him, "the one who's playing the organ? . . ."

"No! the fellow who made it! To economise his notes he hasn't put all of them in the instrument! And that chorus which ought to be played in *La* Major, listen, it's being played in *Doh* major!"

"Well . . . that's a crime! . . ." laughed John Cort.

"And these barbarians who don't notice it . . . Who don't flinch as anyone would flinch who'd got a human ear! . . ."

No! that abomination, the Waggdis did not feel it in all its key for another! . . . If they did not applaud—although they horror! . . . They accepted this criminal substitution of one had enormous hands—their attitude nevertheless showed a complete ecstasy.

"For nothing but that," said Max Huber, "they deserve to be relegated to the rank of the animals."

It was to be presumed that this organ contained no other tunes than the German waltz and the French song, for they followed one another invariably for a whole half-hour. Any other tunes were probably out of order. Fortunately the instrument, which had once possessed all the notes needed for the waltz, did not give to Max Huber the horror which he had felt at the chorus of the song.

When the concert was over the dances were begun more actively than before, and the drinks flowed more abundantly than ever down the Waggdian throats. The sun had just set behind the western treetops, and a few torches shone among the branches so as to illuminate the square, which the short twilight would soon plunge into shadow.

Max Huber and John Cort had had quite enough of it, and they were thinking of going back to their hut when Lo-Maï pronounced that name "Msélo-Tala-Tala."

Was it true? . . . Was His Majesty coming to receive the adoration of his people? . . . Was he deigning at last

JULES VERNE

to emerge from his divine invisibility? . . . John Cort and Max Huber took care not to go away.

And indeed a movement was taking place within the royal hut, and it was replied to by a dull murmur from the audience. The door opened, an escort of warriors formed up, and the Chief Raggi took the head of the procession.

Almost at once there appeared a throne—a sort of litter draped with cloth and foliage—supported by four porters, and on this His Majesty was flaunting himself.

He was a person of about sixty years old, crowned with a wreath, his hair and beard white; he was decidedly corpulent, and his weight must have been heavy on the strong shoulders of his servants.

The procession got into movement, following such a route as to make a tour of the square. The crowd bent towards the earth, as silent as though they were hypnotised by the august presence of Msélo-Tala-Tala.

This monarch seemed quite indifferent, nonetheless, to the homage he was receiving, which was due to him, and to which he was probably accustomed. He scarcely deigned to nod his head in token of satisfaction. Not a gesture except that two or three times he scratched his nose. A long nose surmounted by great spectacles; these justified his surname of "Father-looking-glass."

The two friends stared at him as he passed before them.

"But . . . it's a man!" declared John Cort.

"A man?" replied Max Huber.

"Yes . . . a man . . . and . . . what's more . . . a white man!"

"A white man? . . ."

Yes, it could not be doubted. He who was promenading there on his *sedia gestatoria,* he was a creature different from these Waggdians over whom he reigned, and he was not a native from the tribes of the High Oubanghi . . . Impossible to be mistaken, it was a white man, a qualified representative of the human race! . . .

THE VILLAGE IN THE TREETOPS

"And our presence hasn't had any effect on him," said Max Huber. "And he doesn't seem even to have noticed us! . . . What the devil! We don't look like these semi-apes of Ngala, and because we lived among them for three weeks that doesn't mean, I suppose, that we've lost all human appearance! . . ."

And he was on the point of crying: "Hi . . . Mister . . . you over there, please do us the honour of looking at us . . ."

At that instant John Cort gripped his arm and in a voice which denoted the height of surprise he said, "I can recognise him."

"You recognise him."

"Yes! It's Dr. Johausen!"

CHAPTER XVII

THE CONDITION OF DR. JOHAUSEN

JOHN CORT had previously met Dr. Johausen at Libreville. He could not be mistaken: it was certainly the said doctor who reigned over this Waggdian people! As for his story, nothing could be easier than to sum up its beginning in a few lines and even to reconstitute it completely. Facts unrolled themselves uninterruptedly along that route which stretched from the cage in the forest to Ngala village.

Three years before, this German, anxious to resume the attempts of Professor Garner—which had hardly been serious and which in any case had failed—had left Malimba with an escort of blacks; taking with him equipment, munitions, and food for a fairly long journey. What he wanted to do in the east of the Cameroons everybody knew. He had formed the unlikely project of settling down in the midst of the apes so as to study their language. But in which direction he meant to go, he had not confided that to anyone, being very original and very fussy; to use rather a slang expression, he had a screw loose.

What Khamis and his companions had found during their journey proved incontestibly that the doctor had reached in the forest the river named after him by Max Huber. He had built a raft, and after sending home his escort he had embarked with a native in his service. Then the two had descended the river as far as the marsh at whose end the trellised hut was built beneath the shadow of the trees on the right bank. There ended the certain facts regarding his adventures. As to what had followed, theories were now changed into certitudes.

It will be remembered that Khamis, while ransacking the empty cage, had put his hand on a little box containing a note-book. These notes consisted of a few lines written in pencil, their dates ranging from that of 27th July, 1894, to that of 24th August of the same year.

It was clear then that the doctor had landed on the 9th July, had fixed up his cage on the 13th August, and had stayed in it until the 25th of the same month, thirteen full days in all.

Why had he left it? . . . Was it of his own free will? . . . No, plainly. That the Waggdis sometimes went as far as the banks of the Rio, Khamis and his companions knew quite well. Those flames which had been gleaming at the edge of the forest when the caravan arrived, had they not been carried from tree to tree by these people? . . .

Hence it could be inferred that these primitives had discovered the doctor's hut, that they had seized his person and his equipment and had taken them all to the village in the treetops. As for his native servant, no doubt he had run away through the forest. If he had

THE VILLAGE IN THE TREETOPS

been taken to Ngala John Cort and the others would have met him, for he was not a king and would not have dwelt in the royal hut. Moreover he would have figured in the ceremonies of the day beside his Master as some official, and why not as prime minister? . . .

So the Waggdis had not treated Dr. Johausen any worse than Khamis and his companions. Most probably struck by his intellectual security, they had made him their sovereign—which could have happened to John Cort or Max Huber if the place had not been taken already. So for three years Dr. Johausen, Father-Lookingglass—he himself must have taught that name to his subjects—had occupied the Waggdian throne under the name of Msélo-Tala-Tala.

This explained a number of things hitherto unexplicable; how several words of the Congolese tongue figured in the language of these woodland creatures, as well as two or three words of German; how the use of a barrel-organ was known to them; how they understood how to make certain utensils; how a certain progress had been made in the customs of these types placed on the lowest rung of the human ladder.

That is what these two friends told one another as they went back to their hut. Khamis was at once apprised of the position.

"What I can't understand," Max Huber added, "is that Dr. Johausen didn't seem interested at the presence of foreigners in his capital . . . Why, he hasn't even given orders for us to appear before him! . . . And he didn't seem to have noticed us during the ceremony, though we didn't resemble his subjects at all! . . . Oh, not at all! . . ."

"I quite agree with you, Max," replied John Cort, "and I can't make out why Msélo-Tala-Tala hasn't ordered us to his palace . . ."

"Perhaps he didn't know that the Waggdis had taken prisoners in that part of the forest," suggested the foreloper.

"That's quite possible, but at least it's strange," John Cort declared. "There's something here that eludes me, and that we've got to clear up."

"How?" asked Max Huber.

"If we look hard for it we may find it," John Cort replied.

The inference from all this was that Dr. Johausen came into the Oubanghi Forest to live among the monkeys, had fallen into the hands of a race superior to the apes and whose existence had never been suspected. He had not the trouble of teaching them to speak, because they could speak; he had confined himself to teaching them a few words of the Congolese language and of German. Then in caring for them as a doctor, he must no doubt have acquired a certain popularity which had raised him to the throne! ...

And now what was to be done? ... Dr. Johausen's presence at Ngala, ought it not to modify the position of the prisoners? ... This monarch of Teutonic race, would he hesitate to return them their freedom, if they were to appear before him and ask him to send them back to the Congo? ...

"I can't believe it," said Max Huber, "so our line of action is clear ... it's quite possible that our presence has been concealed from this doctor-king ... I can even admit, no matter how improbable it seems, that during the ceremony he hadn't noticed us in the midst of the crowd ... Well, that's another reason for going into the royal hut."

"When?" John Cort asked him.

"This very evening. And as he's a sovereign whom his people adore, his people will obey him, and when he's set us free, they will take us back to the frontier with the honours due to the fellows of His Waggdian Majesty."

"And if he refuses?"

"Why should he refuse?"

THE VILLAGE IN THE TREETOPS

"Who knows, my dear Max?" laughed John Cort. "For diplomatic reasons, perhaps! ..."

"Well, if he refuses," Max Huber declared, "I shall say that at least he's worthy to reign over the lowest of the monkeys, and that he's below the least of his subjects!"

On the whole, and freed from these fantastic embellishments, the idea was worth taking into consideration. Moreover the opportunity was favourable. If the night had interrupted the festival, what was still continuing, no doubt, was the state of inebriety into which the whole village was plunged ... Must they not take advantage of this circumstance, which perhaps would not recur for some time? ... Of these half-drunken Waggdis some would be asleep in their huts, the others dispersed through the depths of the forest. The very warriors had not been afraid to dishonour their uniform by drinking to their heart's content ... The royal dwelling would be less strictly watched and it should not be difficult to get inside the room of Mséla-Tala-Tala....

This project having been agreed to by Khamis, whose advice was always worth following, they would wait until night had closed down and drunkenness was complete throughout the village. It goes without saying that Kollo, allowed to join the festival, had not come back.

About nine the three men and Llanga went out of their hut. Deprived of all municipal lighting, Ngala was dark. The last gleams of the resinous torches, placed among the trees, had just gone out. In the distance, as though from below Ngala, came a confused noise, on the opposite side from the dwelling of Dr. Johausen.

Foreseeing that it might be possible to get away that very evening, with or without the approval of His Majesty, the three men were provided with their carbines, and all the cartridges from the case filled their pockets. If they were taken by surprise it might be necessary to make these firearms speak—a language which the Waggdis could not possibly know.

The four of them went on between the huts, most of

which were empty. When they reached the darkened square it was deserted. There was only one light, coming from the window of the Royal Hut.

"Nobody," commented John Cort. Indeed nobody, not even in front of the dwelling of Msélo-Tala-Tala.

Raggi and his warriors had forsaken their post, and that night the sovereign would not be well guarded.

There might however be some "chamberlains of service," near His Majesty and it might be hard to escape their surveillance.

Yet Khamis and his companions thought the opportunity very tempting. A lucky chance had enabled them to reach the palace without being noticed, and they felt inclined to go inside.

Climbing along the branches, Llanga could get to the door, and he thought that all that was needed to get through it was a push. The three men at once joined him. For several minutes before going in they listened carefully, ready to beat a retreat if they had to.

No sound could be heard either within or without. Max Huber was the first to cross the threshold. His companions followed him and closed the door behind him.

This building consisted of two continuous rooms which formed Msélo-Tala-Tala's apartment.

Nobody was in the first, which was completely dark.

Khamis looked through the chinks of the door which led into the second room—a badly-jointed door through which came several gleams of light.

Dr. Johausen was there, sprawled on a couch. This article and a few others which furnished the room had evidently come from the cage and had been brought from Ngala at the same time as their owner.

"Let's go in," said Max Huber.

At the noise that they made, Dr. Johausen turned his head and sat up . . . Perhaps he had just been aroused from a deep sleep . . . However this might be,

THE VILLAGE IN THE TREETOPS

the presence of the visitors did not appear to have any effect on him.

"Dr. Johausen, my companions and I have come to offer our homage to Your Majesty!" John Cort addressed him in German.

The Doctor did not reply . . . Had he understood them? . . . Could he have forgotten his own language after three years' stay among the Waggdis?

"Can you hear me?" continued John Cort, "we're foreigners who have been brought to Ngala village . . ."

No reply. These foreigners, the monarch seemed to be looking at them without seeing them, to be listening to them without hearing them. He made no movement, no gesture, as though he were in a state of complete bewilderment.

Max Huber went up to him and, showing little respect towards this monarch of Central Africa, he took him by the shoulders and shook him vigorously.

His Majesty made a face which would not have dishonoured the most grimacing of the Oubanghi apes.

Max Huber shook him again. His Majesty put out his tongue at him.

"Is he mad?" asked John Cort.

"He couldn't be madder, Heaven knows, he's mad enough to be locked up," Max Huber declared.

Yes . . . Dr. Johausen was completely demented. Already partly off his balance when he had left the Cameroons, he had completely lost his reason since arriving at Ngala, and who knew if it were not this mental degeneration which had made him worthy to be proclaimed King of the Waggdis? . . .

The truth is that the poor doctor was devoid of any intellectual power. And that was why he had paid no attention to the presence of the four foreigners in the village, why he had not recognised in two of them individuals of his own species, so very different from the Waggdians!

"There's only one thing to do," said Khamis. "We

can't count on the intervention of this poor creature to set us free . . ."

"Certainly not!" John Cort declared.

"And those animals out there won't let us go . . ." Max Huber added. "So, as we've got an opportunity to escape, let's take it."

"This very instant," Khamis insisted, "let's take advantage of the darkness . . ."

"And the condition of all this world of semi-apes . . ." Max Huber agreed.

"Come on," said Khamis as he made for the outer chamber. "Let's try to reach the stairway and we'll make off across the forest . . ."

"Agreed," replied Max Huber, "but . . . the doctor . . ."

"The doctor?" repeated Khamis.

"We can't let him stay in his kingdom! . . . It's our duty to set him free . . ."

"Yes, certainly, my dear Max," John Cort agreed, "but this poor wretch has lost his wits . . . he may resist . . . and if he refuses to follow us? . . ."

"We must try it anyway," Max Huber replied as he went up to the doctor.

That fat man—it may well be imagined—would not be easy to move and if he did not agree how could they ever get him out of the hut? . . .

Khamis and John Cort went to the aid of Max Huber, and gripped the doctor by the arm.

The latter, still quite strong, thrust them away and fell back at full length on his bed, moving his arms and legs like a lobster which had been turned on its back.

"Dr. Johausen?" John Cort cried for the last time.

His Majesty Mséla-Tala-Tala's only response was to scratch himself in a very monkey-like fashion . . .

"Certainly," said Max Huber, "there's nothing to be got from this human beast! . . . He's become a monkey . . . Let him stay a monkey and go on reigning over these monkeys in peace!"

THE VILLAGE IN THE TREETOPS

The only thing to do was to leave the royal dwelling. Unfortunately while he was making contortions His Majesty had begun to call out, and so loudly that he must have been heard if there had been any of the Waggdis in the neighbourhood.

Moreover, to lose even a few seconds would be to risk missing so favourable an opportunity . . . maybe Raggi and his warriors would have come running up . . . The position of the foreigners, surprised in the dwelling of Msélo-Tala-Tala, would be much worse and they would have to give up any hope of regaining their liberty . . . So Khamis and his comrades abandoned Dr. Johausen, and, opening the door, they dashed outside.

CHAPTER XVIII

SUDDEN CONCLUSION

CHANCE FAVOURED the fugitives. All that din inside the hut had not attracted anyone. The square was deserted, and so were the streets which led up to it. But the difficulty would be to find out where they were in the midst of that dark maze, to make their way among its windings, to reach by the shortest route the staircase from Ngala.

Suddenly Lo-Maï appeared before Khamis and his companions; he was accompanied by his child. The boy, who had followed them while they went to the hut of Msélo-Tala-Tala, had gone to warn his father. The latter, dreading some danger to the foreloper and his companions, hastened to join them. Realising that they wanted to get away, he was going to act as their guide.

This was lucky, for none of them would have been able to find the path to the stairway.

But when they reached it what was their disappointment! The entrance was guarded by Raggi and a dozen of his warriors. To force their way through, all four of them, would they have any possible hope of success? . . .

Max Huber thought that the moment had come to use his carbine. Raggi and two others were about to throw themselves upon him . . .

Retiring a few paces, he opened fire on the group.

Raggi, hit right in the chest, fell stone dead.

The Waggdis certainly knew neither the use of firearms nor their effects. The explosion and Raggi's fall gave them a fright of which nobody could form any idea. A thunderbolt striking the square during the day's ceremony would have frightened them less. The group of warriors scattered, some going back into the village, the others swarming down the staircase with the agility of apes. In an instant the way was clear.

"Down there!" shouted Khamis.

All he had to do was to follow Lo-Maï and the child, who went before him. The three men and Llanga almost let themselves slide down without meeting any obstacle. After passing beneath the village they made for the bank of the river, reached it in a few minutes, unmoored one of the canoes and embarked with the father and the child.

But then torches were flaming out everywhere, and from everywhere were running a great crowd of those Waggdis who had been wandering near the village. Shouts of anger and threats were supported by a cloud of arrows. "Come on," said John Cort, "we've got to!"

He and Max Huber raised their carbines, while Khamis and Llanga succeeded in driving the canoe from the shore.

A double explosion rang out. Two Waggdis were hit and the howling crowd scattered.

At that moment the canoe was gripped by the cur-

THE VILLAGE IN THE TREETOPS

rent and vanished down-stream beneath the shade of the great trees.

* * * *

There is no need to report—at least in any detail—the course of that navigation towards the south-west of the great forest. If there were any other treetop villages, the two friends knew nothing about them. As there was no shortage of munitions, their food was assured by what they could get by hunting, various sorts of antelopes abounding in that region. Next evening Khamis moored the canoe to a tree on the bank for the night.

During this journey, John Cort and Max Huber had not been sparing of tokens of gratitude to Lo-Maï, for whom they felt quite a human sympathy. As for Llanga and the child, a real brotherly friendship had sprung up between them. How could he feel the differences in type which placed him above this little creature?

John Cort and Max Huber had hoped that Lo-Maï would go with them back to Libreville. The return journey should be easy in going down that rio, which ought to be one of the tributaries of the Oubanghi. The essential thing was that its course should not be obstructed either by rapids or by waterfalls.

It was on the evening of 16th April that the canoe had stopped, after a journey of fifteen hours. Khamis estimated that thirty to forty miles had been covered since the previous night.

It was agreed that the night should be spent there. When camp had been organised and the meal was over, Lo-Maï kept watch while the others slept a refreshing sleep which was not disturbed in any way.

When they awoke Khamis got ready to set out, and all that had to be done was to launch the canoe into the current.

At that moment Lo-Maï, who was holding his child

JULES VERNE

by his hand, was waiting on the bank. John Cort and Max Huber joined him and pressed him to follow them. Lo-Maï shook his head and pointed with one hand down-stream and with the other to the thick depths of the forest.

The two friends insisted, and their gestures were sufficient to make them understood. They wanted to take Lo-Maï and Li-Maï to Libreville ...

Meantime Llanga was lavishing caresses on the child, kissing him, hugging him in his arms ... he wanted to drag him into the canoe ...

Li-Maï said only the one word: *"Ngora!"*

Yes ... his mother who had stayed in the village and to whom his father and he wished to return ... It was a family which nothing could separate!

The last farewells were made, after the food supply of Lo-Maï and the child had been assured for their journey back to Ngala.

John Cort and Max Huber did not hide their emotion at the thought that they would never again see these good affectionate creatures, however inferior their race might be. ... As for Llanga, he could not keep from crying, and great tears were also moistening the eyes of father and son.

"Well," said John Cort, "now do you believe, my dear Max, that these poor creatures have some links with humanity? ..."

"Yes, John, because, just like men, they have smiles and tears!"

The canoe was caught by the current and at the bend in the bank Khamis and his companions could wave a last farewell to Lo-Maï and his son.

The days from 17th to 26th April were spent in descending the river to its confluence with the Oubanghi. Its current being very swift, they estimated at about 250 miles the distance they had covered since leaving Ngala village.

They were then at the height of the Zongo rapids,

THE VILLAGE IN THE TREETOPS

near the bend which the river takes when it swerves towards the south. It would be impossible to cross these rapids in the canoe, and to continue navigation downstream a portage would be necessary. Certainly, their route allowed them to follow the left bank of the Oubanghi on foot. But to that painful journey the canoe would have been infinitely preferable. Would it not have been time gained and fatigue spared? ...

Fortunately, Khamis was able to avoid this troublesome portage.

Below the Zongo rapids the Oubanghi is navigable down to its junction with the Congo. Boats are by no means scarce in that region, where neither villages nor townships nor missionary establishments are lacking. The 400 miles which separated them from their goal the four men were able to traverse on board one of these large boats, which were towed by steam tugs.

It was on 28th April that they stopped near to a township on the right bank. Recovered from their fatigue and in good condition, it would only take them 700 miles to reach Libreville. A caravan was at once organised under the care of the foreloper, and, travelling directly westwards, it traversed these vast Congo plains in twenty-four days.

On the 20th May, John Cort, Max Huber, Khamis and Llanga entered the factory near the town. Here their friends, very uneasy at so prolonged an absence, with no news of them for nearly six months, welcomed them with open arms.

Neither Khamis nor the young native could separate from John Cort and Max Huber. Had they not adopted Llanga, and had not the foreloper been their devoted guide throughout that adventurous journey? ...

And Dr. Johausen? ... And the Treetops Village of Ngala, lost in the depths of the great forest? ...

Well, sooner or later, some expedition must make with these strange Waggdis a more intimate contact in the interests of modern anthropological science.

As for the German doctor, he is mad, and even supposing that he regained his reason and that they took him back to Malimba, who knows if he would not regret the time during which he had reigned under the name of Msélo-Tala-Tala? Who knows whether, thanks to him, this primitive people will not pass one day under the protectorate of the German Empire? . . .

But it is always possible that England . . .

THE FITZROY EDITION OF
JULES VERNE

The intention of this new edition of one of the greatest of imaginative writers is to make it as comprehensive as possible, and to include his lesser-known, as well as his most popular works. Jules Verne is universally acclaimed as the founder of modern science-fiction and as the author of many exciting stories of travel and adventure, but he also produced several fine historical novels and some acute studies of contemporary life.

Ace Books has contracted with the publishers to produce this series in its entirety under their authorization and that of the series' distinguished editor. The books have been modernized for uniform presentation and in many cases have been translated into English for the first time.

I. O. Evans, Fellow of the Royal Geographical Society, has been for many years an admirer of Jules Verne and a devotee of science-fiction.

CLASSICS OF GREAT SCIENCE-FICTION

from ACE BOOKS

M-154	(45¢)	**INVADERS FROM THE INFINITE** by John W. Campbell
F-422	(40¢)	**SWORD OF RHIANNON** by Leigh Brackett
F-426	(40¢)	**THE GENETIC GENERAL** by Gordon R. Dickson
G-627	(50¢)	**THE BIG TIME** by Fritz Leiber
G-634	(50¢)	**WAR OF THE WING-MEN** by Poul Anderson
M-165	(45¢)	**WORLDS OF THE IMPERIUM** by Keith Laumer
G-649	(50¢)	**THE WORLD SWAPPERS** by John Brunner
G-661	(50¢)	**BIG PLANET** by Jack Vance
H-30	(60¢)	**CITY** by Clifford D. Simak
G-676	(50¢)	**THE SECRET VISITORS** by James White
G-683	(50¢)	**THE BIG JUMP** by Leigh Brackett
H-39	(60¢)	**EYE IN THE SKY** by Philip K. Dick
G-697	(50¢)	**WE CLAIM THESE STARS** by Poul Anderson
G-706	(50¢)	**THE JEWELS OF APTOR** by Samuel R. Delany
G-718	(50¢)	**SOLAR LOTTERY** by Philip K. Dick

Available from Ace Books, Inc. (Dept. MM), 1120 Avenue of the Americas, New York, N.Y. 10036. Send price indicated, plus 10¢ handling fee.